PENGUIN BOOKS
THERE WAS NO ONE AT THE BUS STOP

SIRSHENDU MUKHOPADHYAY is one of Bengal's most admired contemporary fiction writers. Bursting on to the scene with his first novel, *Ghunpoka* (Woodworm), he stamped his presence with searingly uncompromising portrayals of darkness and frailty in human beings. His exploration of the seamier side of relationships and existence, his versatility of canvas and his spare but charged writing style make him an undisputed star of Bengali literature. He lives and writes in Kolkata.

ARUNAVA SINHA is an Internet professional by day and a translator of classic and contemporary fiction by late night. His published translations include Sankar's *Chowringhee* (2007) and *The Middleman* (2009), Buddhadeva Bose's *My Kind of Girl* (2009) and Moti Nandy's *Striker Stopper* (2010). Born and educated in Kolkata, he now lives in New Delhi.

There Was No One at the Bus Stop

SIRSHENDU MUKHOPADHYAY

Translated from the Bengali by

ARUNAVA SINHA

PENGUIN BOOKS

PENGUIN BOOKS
Published by the Penguin Group
Penguin Books India Pvt. Ltd, 11 Community Centre, Panchsheel Park,
New Delhi 110017, India
Penguin Group (USA) Inc., 375 Hudson Street, New York, New York 10014,
USA
Penguin Group (Canada), 90 Eglinton Avenue East, Suite 700, Toronto,
Ontario, M4P2Y3, Canada (a division of Pearson Penguin Canada Inc.)
Penguin Books Ltd, 80 Strand, London WC2R 0RL, England
Penguin Ireland, 25 St Stephen's Green, Dublin 2, Ireland (a division of
Penguin Books Ltd)
Penguin Group (Australia), 250 Camberwell Road, Camberwell, Victoria
3124, Australia (a division of Pearson Australia Group Pty Ltd)
Penguin Group (NZ), 67 Apollo Drive, Rosedale, North Shore 0632,
New Zealand (a division of Pearson New Zealand Ltd)
Penguin Group (South Africa) (Pty) Ltd, 24 Sturdee Avenue, Rosebank,
Johannesburg 2196, South Africa

Penguin Books Ltd, Registered Offices: 80 Strand, London WC2R 0RL, England

First published in Bengali as *Bus Stop-e Keu Nei* by Ananda Publishers 1974
First published by Penguin Books India 2010

Copyright © Sirshendu Mukhopadhyay 1974, 2010
Translation copyright © Arunava Sinha 2010

All rights reserved

10 9 8 7 6 5 4 3 2 1

This is a work of fiction. Names, characters, places and incidents are either the
product of the author's imagination or are used fictitiously, and any resemblance
to actual persons, living or dead, events, or locales is entirely coincidental.

ISBN 9780143067733

Typeset in Goudy Old Style by Eleven Arts, New Delhi
Printed at Replika Press Pvt. Ltd, Sonipat

A s he was about to leave his room, sleep still clinging to his eyes, Robi gingerly parted the curtains leading to the next room and saw his father. Smoke rose from behind *The Statesman*, while a pair of feet were visible on a small stool, a steaming cup of coffee next to them. That *Statesman*, those feet and the coffee-cup—that was his father. Robi pulled out his toy revolver from the pockets of his shorts. Raising it, he squinted, aimed and pulled the trigger.

Bang! Bang! Bang! Three bullets were fired in the twinkling of an eye. *The Statesman* was the first to drop to the ground, after which his father slumped to the luxurious soft foam sofa with expensive springs, his body rolling. He emitted a convincing death rattle—Aaaaaaah aah aah aah . . .

Robi smiled. Putting the revolver back in his pocket, he advanced a couple of steps. Without getting up, his father Debashish looked at him and said, Shot! Shot!

A suppressed but enigmatic smile played on Robi's young, sleepy face. Nice of you to say that, he said.

Debashish sat up, putting his glowing cigarette back to his lips. Proceed towards the bathroom, he said, before hiding behind *The Statesman* again.

Yeah, yawned Robi. Didi, he called.

Parting the curtains on the door to the other room, Champa, the maid who was halfway to being an old woman, answered instantly with a smile, Sweetheart!

Stretching his arms, Robi said sleepily, Ride.

Champa picked him up. Robi hated this first visit of the morning to the toilet. He spent a few minutes in Champa's arms every morning, yawning with his head on her shoulders.

It's Sunday, Champa whispered.

Hmm.

Holiday.

Yeah.

Where's my darling going with Baba today?

An exquisite smile lit up Robi's soft young face. Champa drew the curtains of the wide window with its huge windowpanes. The view from the sixth floor, of a sprawling Calcutta, came to life like a painting. There was a large park directly below them, a lake in the middle. People were walking on the paved path around it.

The phone rang in the next room, followed by the click of the receiver being taken off the cradle. Hello, came Debashish's voice.

Phone, said Robi.

Hmm, said Champa.

Can you tell me who's calling?

Some friend of your father's.

No, it's Monima.

Champa's face lost its smile. Come along, brush your teeth now, she said.

You didn't finish last night's story, Robi yawned.

I will, smiled Champa, while you brush your teeth.

Debashish could be heard laughing. Today? he said. Hmm . . . Hmm . . . No, Sunday is for Robi alone. I spend the entire day with him. Okay . . .

Agog, Robi listened. Definitely Monima, he said.

Come along now.

Robi yawned as he urinated in the toilet. Champa was about to squeeze the toothpaste out on to his tiny toothbrush when he said angrily, No paste!

What'll you brush your teeth with, then?

Your black toothpowder.

That's spicy. The paste is sweet.

No, the paste's horrible. The foam makes me puke.

Your father will be very angry if he gets to know you used my toothpowder.

How will he know? Brush my teeth quietly now. With your fingers. The toothbrush is horrible.

An affectionate smile appeared on Champa's aged face.

3

Fetching her cheap black toothpowder from the kitchen, she cleaned Robi's teeth with it.

What about the story? Robi frowned.

Oh yes. Then the . . . where were we, sweetheart?

You can never remember. Shibucharan had gone fishing alone in his boat at night. In his net he found a cobra along with the fish.

That's right. As soon as he unfurled the net by the light of a lantern a cobra appeared along with the fish. His boat was small, no more than four feet or so in length. Shibucharan stood at one end, his mouth fallen open; the lantern glowed in the middle; and the cobra raised its hood at the other end. And the fish, still alive, were thrashing about in the hull. There was inky black darkness everywhere, and not a sound to be heard. What a pickle Shibucharan was in, there in the middle of the river. He just couldn't move, paralysed both in his brain and in his limbs by fear.

Rinsing his mouth out, Robi asked, Why didn't he jump into the river?

Champa paused in mid-flow, taken aback. Wide-eyed, she said, You're right, sweetheart! So small, but how clever! Oh my god!

Wiping his face with a towel, Champa cradled him in her arms again. Holding his head to her shoulder, she said, My sweetheart is so sharp. I've never seen anyone so clever.

Smiling proudly, Robi hid his face in her shoulder. Then? What happened after that?

Yes, so Shibucharan was rooted to the spot. He was trembling. I'm about to die, he thought. I'll never see my family and children again. The snake will get me. Help, someone! But there was no one close by. There wasn't a soul mid-river in the middle of the winter night. Shibucharan realized it was no use crying out for help. No one could hear him. In sheer fright he started reeling off the names of the gods, but the snake didn't budge. Shibu realized he was getting it wrong, so he focused on the snake goddess alone. But that seemed to excite the cobra further. It struck with its fangs a couple of times. The lantern would save him, but for how long? Shibu realised the snake goddess wasn't happy with him for some reason. No use asking her for help, it was making things worse. Then Shibucharan remembered that the village priest did say that the spirits of your ancestors . . . Sit down now, sweetheart.

Carrying Robi into the dining room, Champa made him sit down at the table. Annoyed, Robi clung to her, saying, Sit on the chair, I'm going to sit in your lap.

Looking around, Champa said, How can I sit on the chair? Your father will be angry if he sees me.

He won't be angry at all. Oh, sit down now. Why don't you listen to me?

All right, all right. Champa sat down, pulling him onto her lap. Pritam, the servant, brought a plate of buttered toast and a glass of milk. Robi-babu, he asked grimly, when I was asleep last evening, may I know who poured water into my ear and ran away?

And why do you sleep evenings? Don't you know Baba gets angry?

I wasn't sleeping, just thinking up a story for you with my eyes shut when you poured the water in and ran away. It's still sloshing round in my earhole. I'm going to tell your father today, see if I don't.

Pulling his toy revolver out of his pocket solemnly, Robi pressed the trigger.

Bang! Bang! Bang!

Aaaaaah aah aah, said Pritam and left the room, stumbling like someone who has been shot.

And then? said Robi, sipping his milk.

Where was I? asked Champa helplessly.

You never remember.

I'm getting old, you see.

Does getting old mean you have to forget everything?

Putting her cheek against his for an instant, Champa drew back. The priest always said, The spirits of our ancestors keep an eye on you constantly. They can't do anything by themselves, but if you call on them with all your heart, they come and rescue you from danger. So Shibucharan started calling on them—Forefathers mine, wherever you are, come quick, see what your favourite Shibu has landed himself in. Who's going to even realize in the dead of night that Shibu's been bitten by a venomous creature? Who's going to call the doctor? Shibu's a goner—he was muttering things like this when the snake suddenly spoke in a human voice, Hey Shibucharan—

Parting the curtains, Debashish appeared from the next room. Hurry up, hurry up! he said in a slightly deep voice.

Gee, Robi grinned, turning his face. Champa rose awkwardly, still holding Robi.

Debashish smiled at the scene, and drew the curtains closed again. His voice could be heard from the next room, Get dressed, get dressed quickly.

Yeah, answered Robi. After two bites of his toast, he said, Quick, Didi.

You've hardly eaten, sweetheart!

I don't feel like.

Just two sips of the milk, please!

How you trouble me!

Robi gulped down his milk. Wiping his mouth with the back of his hand, he ran into his room, saying, Quick, Didi!

Debashish shut the door carefully. Robi was getting dressed in the other room. It was 8 a.m. Trina must have woken up by now. She wasn't an early riser. Debashish pictured the scene at her house right now. Sachin, Trina's husband, was in his garden which was just across the road from their house, and where, by this time of the morning, he was completely absorbed. You rarely saw a person so obsessed with flowers, so besotted with his garden. He wouldn't sell their 5000 square feet of prime land on Hazra Road, despite marvellous offers, just because of that garden. They didn't need those 5000 square feet at all, for their house already stood on huge grounds. Trina had one son and one daughter—Manu and Reba. Manu went for tennis classes on Sunday, while Reba had dancing and singing lessons. Between eight and quarter past eight, there wasn't anyone around Trina except for the servants. Not that it mattered. Everyone knew of the *plus sign* between Debashish and Trina. In fact, the cloud of suspicion over whether Debashish's wife Chandana had committed suicide or been murdered had not yet lifted. The police did bring the case to court, and tried to implicate Debashish as a murderer, though the case was too weak to be sustained. Nonetheless, in the court of public opinion Debashish was probably still tainted.

The ringing began precisely after he dialled the number, and Debashish missed two heartbeats. He had difficulty breathing.

Hello, said Trina.

Deb.

I know.

Can you talk?

Not really.

Someone in the room?

Hmm.

I'll telephone you back in ten minutes, then.

Trina laughed. No, she said, who would be around at this hour? It's Sunday, for one thing, and then you have the autumn sunshine with the rains gone. I'm all by myself. There's no one here.

What were you doing?

Book of Jibanananda's poems in my hand, telephone by my side. But I haven't read a single poem yet.

Debashish cleared his throat. What're you planning to do today?

What do you suppose? Nothing. You?

Robi doesn't want to spend Sundays with Champa these days.

He's getting older, after all, blood will tell. You're his father, remember?

Not going out?

Trina sighed. You know how it is, there's this barbed wire of disapproval all around me. If I go out by myself Sachin looks at me very strangely. The older he's getting, the more suspicious he's becoming. The children don't like it either. So I keep to my room.

Nonsense. What kind of life is that?

Then what kind of life would sir prefer?

What I'd suggest is: go out. So will I.

And then?

We'll meet somewhere.

After a pause, Trina said, Deb, Robi's growing up.

So?

Be careful. Don't let your child be a witness.

Tinu, you never used to be so conservative. What's happening to you?

I'm getting older.

I don't know all that. I haven't seen you in a week.

Liar.

What do you mean?

I'm saying you're a liar, Trina laughed.

Why?

Just two days ago you were parked at a spot on the road from where you could see my bedroom window.

Debashish clutched his chest with his left hand. Trouble breathing. Missed heartbeats . . . One . . . Two. He breathed again. Inhaled a huge lungful of air.

How did you know it was me? he asked, speaking slowly.

Because I can always tell it's you.

You must have seen the number-plate.

No. I could barely see the car. All I could see was a glowing cigarette and two burning eyes.

Rubbish.

I know Deb, it could have been nobody but you.

Debashish clenched his teeth and shut his eyes, drowning in his own embarrassment. His voice seemed to be someone else's as he said, No one else but you got to know, right?

How can anyone else? Trina laughed. How can someone who doesn't know you even imagine whose car it is that's parked on the road? Who's sitting alone in the driver's seat like a ghost? Who else but me is even bothered?

You stood at the large window for a long time. The light was behind you, so I couldn't make out your face. If only I'd known you could see me.

What would you have done?

I'd have danced a jig on the road.

Deb, you're growing older, not younger.

And madder, not saner.

I can see that. But why? Why do you need to park yourself like a beggar next to my house. We're not new.

Debashish couldn't find an answer. His blood roared in his chest. An unstoppable force seemed to hammer against his ribcage. I'm very greedy, Tinu, he said.

Greedy or not, you're definitely groping. In the dark.

Meaning?

Meaning stupid. Got it?

And why?

Where's Robi? Can he hear all this madness?

What if he can? He's too young to understand.

Smiling, Trina said, You know nothing about children. They're very precocious these days. Besides, children understand everything.

Listen, there's no need to worry about Robi, said Debashish, a bit hopelessly. There's no point, either. If he does find out, let him. Tell me first whether we're meeting or not.

Where? asked Trina softly.

Wherever you want.

I'm embarrassed. Your son will be with you.

It's not as if he doesn't know you. When did you start developing these new inhibitions?

I worry because Robi's growing up. He's learning things.

Don't worry. I'm taking the car. We'll spend an hour or so at the zoo and the restaurant. My sister has invited us to lunch. Actually only Robi is invited, I'm not very popular at her place, as you know. I'm free once I've dropped Robi there.

That means eleven or twelve o' clock. Do you suppose I'm as independent as you are, Deb? What will people say if I'm out when it's time for everyone to have their lunch?

Then come to the zoo or the restaurant.

Then Robi will definitely see me.

Oh, you raise too many objections.

All right, let's stick to the programme for the afternoon, laughed Trina. Where?

How about the bus stop at Ballygunge?

Out of the corner of his eye, Debashish saw Robi at the threshold of the room, the curtains parted. He was dressed in light blue shorts and a milk-white T-shirt, with the first letter of his name monogrammed near his left breast. His hair was curly and clumped. The slight smile on his face was now fading gradually.

Well then? said Debashish into the phone.

Bye then.

So long.

He put the phone down.

The smile had been wiped off Robi's face—he was looking at his father. He turned his face away as soon as their eyes met.

Debashish looked at his son. The storm in his breast had abated, the waves had subsided. There was only tiredness now. This was how it was after the tension had ended. It was difficult to put on an easy smile; the tug-of-war hadn't quite finished yet. He would meet Trina in the afternoon, at the bus stop at Ballygunge. His nerves still felt parched with longing—anxious. They would meet, their thirst would deepen, but there would still be an ocean between Trina and him all their lives.

When Robi looked up, Debashish gave him a tortured smile. Did Robi know everything? A sudden fear gripped his heart.

Debashish smartly took a step forward, holding out his hand and saying, I'm Debashish Dasgupta.

Shaking the hand he held out, Robi said, I'm Navin Dasgupta, pleased to meet you.

Champa stood behind Robi. She was dressed in a clean sari, her hair neatly combed. As soon as Debashish looked at her she said, Should I come along?

Where? asked Debashish in surprise.

He's refusing to listen, insisting I come along, said Champa shyly.

Can Didi come, Baba? wheedled Robi.

She can if you want her to, said Debashish with a slight smile. But where will she have lunch? She hasn't been invited.

Champa's face lit up with a smile. I won't eat anything, I had some rice in the morning. If I can stay with my darling, that's enough for me.

Nodding distractedly, Debashish twirled the car keys round his fingers as he headed towards the lift.

L ove was one thing, sin was another—and although it was difficult to tell love from sin, Trina had learnt to identify some of the signs.

When she thought of Debashish, she felt uncomfortable looking at Sachin. She couldn't look at her children either. An arid wind seemed to blow in her breast, her tongue dried up, she looked around furtively without reason. She even feared her own shadow.

Emerging from the bathroom after her shower, Trina was startled. It was just Sachin, washing his hands, muddied from his gardening, at the washbasin outside. A short, compact man of about forty-two, Sachin was quite well built and his appearance reflected a stern male beauty. Although Sachin didn't even glance at her, Trina had to clutch at the bathroom door to support herself. She had her sari loosely wrapped around her. Feeling exposed, she fumbled with the sari to cover the bare parts of her body and, face averted, entered her room.

The room was hers, entirely hers. An enormous bed to one side, bookshelves within reach of the bed, a dressing-table on the other side, a wardrobe, a cupboard—all of it expensive furniture. Through two large windows, the autumnal morning sunshine flooded the floor, glaring in its brightness. She put on her everyday undergarments and blouse, draped the sari properly around herself, and then, taking a formal sari and matching blouse out of the wardrobe, put them on the bed. Turning back to examine them from a distance, she sat down before the mirror. She was slim, fair, possibly attractive in appearance, but her most engaging quality was the vivacity in her face. Her eyes talked, her eyes laughed, her nostrils trembled at the slightest of emotions. Her lips were full, as were her cheeks, and all told, she looked much younger than her age. It was obvious that she had not really lacked for anything all these years. Trina loved herself, because she could be loved. Sometimes she fell in love with herself.

Sachin could be heard in the next room. He had a habit of humming tunelessly. It wasn't an actual song, though it resembled one. This was the one habit he had. Was this tuneless humming the sound of his loneliness?

If that were so, Trina alone wasn't responsible for that loneliness. Nor was Debashish. Once upon a time Sachin had meant everything to Trina. But was Trina part of Sachin's life now? She listened avidly to his humming. The door between their rooms stayed shut at night; a heavy satin curtain hung in place during the day. Sachin didn't spend much time in his room, however, but when he did, that heavy curtain remained drawn, unmoving. Neither of them entered the other's room. The children lived in another corner of the house. She didn't run into them casually either. And even when she did, there was very little conversation. Only during meals was Trina present. But even that seemed like a hushed memorial service. Everyone ate in silence. Tears pricked Trina's eyes, but what use were they? When even a weapon as powerful as tears failed, one had nothing left. For all intents and purposes, one wasn't even present any more. Just as Trina was no longer present in this house—in this household. She was no more than a dead person in a framed photo on the wall. Thus, Trina was not responsible.

She patted her neck and shoulders with the soft powder-puff, put the sindoor in her hair, took a little cream and rubbed it into her cheeks. There was nothing more to do now. She didn't actually have much to do all day. The cook took two thousand rupees a month, which implied there was nothing to teach him. The servants and maids who kept the house clean and organized also knew their work well. Trina only walked around, supervising them. Sometimes she cooked something herself. Nobody cared much for what she cooked; Trina too had forgotten her culinary skills. All she did was give instructions and her instructions were followed. Only in her own room did she arrange her own books, make her bed herself, organize her wardrobe, set out her cosmetics on her dressing table according to her own wishes, clean the mirror with a moistened piece of paper. People didn't come into this room very often. This was her own room. Far too empty, far too large. There was a large balcony looking out on to the road, and she stood in it sometimes like a spectre. Her companions through the day were volumes of poetry, magazines, novels and short stories, watercolours, thick paper, paintbrushes. Recently she had started writing poetry, sending one or two to magazines now and then. The poems were full of melancholia, ponderous in their loneliness, emotionally overloaded with personal regrets—none of them had been published yet. She wouldn't have minded if one or two had been published. The watercolours she had painted were mostly sceneries. Palm trees, a river with a boat in it— the easiest paintings ever. Followed by mountains. Trina hadn't really learnt how to draw, nor had she been trained to wield watercolours and brushes. The paintings often got smudged, but still she painted. She thought she might have an exhibition at the Academy of Fine Arts or Birla Museum. Not that it would serve any purpose. No one would bother. She didn't even know the basics of art. Trina used to be a good carrom-player in college. There were two enormous carrom boards at home. Sometimes she arranged the pieces and used a striker to pot them. But without an opponent, there was no tension in the game, and she tired of it easily.

How long can you go on playing against yourself, playing with white from this side and black from that?

Sachin kept humming a tuneless, wordless song in the next room. Having inherited his wealth, he hadn't had to go through the grind of establishing himself. Most of the hard work had already been done by his father. Even after splitting their father's enormous estate between the four of them, all the brothers were still wealthy. The house had fallen into Sachin's share. His elder brother had taken the cement business, and of the two younger brothers, one had taken the pharmacy and the other, the blue-chip investments. All four brothers were well qualified. Sachin himself was an engineer, with an important job in a big company. He had been abroad twice—once at the company's expense, and once at his own. He had visited almost every country in the world, other than China and Russia. Which woman wouldn't be thrilled with such a husband and such a family? Powerfully built and somewhat dispassionate, Sachin loved flowers and beautiful colours, as well as philosophy and discourse. He was interested in people. Yet, on these holidays or in his spare time—when he gardened, or casually flipped through journals in his room, or hummed—he seemed rather lazy.

That's why Trina hated it at home on holidays. It was one thing to be alone by oneself, but quite another thing altogether to feel lonely even in the company of others.

It was rather a strange household. Not a thing ever fell to the floor, nothing was ever broken, the milk never boiled over, the food was never burnt. Everything was run efficiently. Trina was superfluous. There were two dogs—an Alsatian and a boxer. They weren't to be seen or heard either. Only Sachin's aged parrot talked precociously. But its words were learnt sounds, lifeless. Without comprehending the meaning, the bird cried, Come, Trina, come, Trina.

The bird had grown old. It would die one day. There'd be no one to call out to Trina after that.

No, there would be someone. Debashish. He was quite mad. He called to her in a way that made everyone know of it. Sachin knew, the children too. Trina's heart trembled all the time. Sometimes in the excitement of a forbidden relationship. Sometimes in fear. Sachin and the children didn't consider her any better than a whore. And Debashish? Did he think of her as anything but a fallen woman?

The parrot called. Trina had an urge to pet the bird. The huge cage hung in the balcony outside Sachin's room. She would have to go through his room to get there. She could have, had he not been there. But the tuneless humming could still be heard in the other room. She always thought of herself as an immoral woman in his presence these days. It was such agony. Sachin didn't say anything to her any more because he was a gentleman. About six months ago, he had lost his patience and slapped her, even given her a few blows with his cane. He must have felt remorseful ever since. But how could Trina let him know that her memory of that thrashing was a pleasurable one even now. For her conscience and her heart constantly expected punishment.

Picking up the book that was lying face-down on her desk, Trina began reading it. It was a volume of poetry which she had read many times. She knew the poems by heart. Still she gazed at the sonnet on the open page. Unable to concentrate, she put the book aside and drew pen and paper to herself. Uncapping the pen, she hunched over the paper, the pen poised impatiently, restlessly, before she moved it. But she wasn't able to write anything. She drew a few thin, tall figures, then started scribbling and doodling gibberish all over the sheet before scrunching it up and throwing it away. Then she scribbled and doodled again on a fresh sheet.

The parrot called, Sachin, Sachin, stop thief, Sachin, stop thief.

Sachin's room was silent now. Trina rose and peeped in. There was no one in there. The room was neatly done up. Sachin had refurbished and even rebuilt parts of the house, which dated back to his father's time. It was to renovate the house that Debashish had been appointed. He was the managing director of the civil draughtsmanship and interior decorating firm Indec. Managing director was too weighty a term for a company like Indec, which was not all that big. There were hundreds of companies like that in Calcutta. Yet,

Indec had something of a reputation. Besides interiors, they took on small projects for construction or renovation. They designed plans for new buildings too. They got business precisely because they could offer so many different services. Debashish Dasgupta had been an artist once, earning quite a name for himself in commercial art. But with ambition taking over, he had spent some time directing films. Eventually he had managed to settle into interior decoration. Since he was an artist with a unique eye for colour and design, and because of his earlier goodwill, it hadn't taken him long to establish himself. He now had an office in Chowringhee, employing a civil engineer, two draughtsmen, and several other professionals, including a female receptionist. His personal chamber was air-conditioned, and he lived in a flat he had bought for himself. He flaunted a Morris Oxford car.

But this was today's Debashish, in whom it was well-nigh impossible to discover the older Debashish.

The day that he came to take the brief for the renovation, Debashish had parked his car outside and accompanied Sachin with careful footsteps, surveying the house. His eyes held an aggressive hunger, his gait the hallmark of a busy man in a hurry. Sachin was showing him around the house— identifying the spots where the wall would have to be broken down for a balcony, where the tiles would have to be replaced, where new rooms would have to be added, how the interiors would have to be designed to transform an old house into a contemporary one. The haughty Trina had spared only a negligent half-glance for the tall, well-built man with Sachin, not noticing him at all. It was Sachin who had called her— Trina, will you explain your plans to Dasgupta here . . .

They had sat down to tea, Debashish directly opposite her. After a quick glance at him, Trina was about to lower her eyes in order to sketch a plan for the study on a pad, when Debashish—having stared at her for a few moments—said a trifle abruptly and stupidly, Trina, right?

Trina was startled. It took her some effort to recognize Debashish. It meant going all the way back to her childhood, so naturally it needed some effort.

You know her? asked Sachin.

Looking at her with wide eyes, Debashish said, It certainly wasn't easy identifying her. Trina wasn't even supposed to be alive any more. She used to be so ill, we had thought she would have died by now.

Really, smiled Sachin.

Of course, said Debashish in surprise. We were neighbours in our small town. I know everything about her. When we were young, she was constantly bedridden. At best she'd come out as far as the veranda or the courtyard and watch everyone else play. Sometimes it was dysentery that she was about to die of, sometimes typhoid, sometimes pneumonia. But she survived them all, ticking over somehow. When we moved away, she was probably suffering from malaria. My mother often used to say, I doubt if Madan-babu's second daughter has long to live.

Trina was very embarrassed. She used to be ill all the time. But all that was in childhood, she protested.

I haven't seen you since. Do you even recognize me?

I do.

Who am I, then?

Rajen-jyatha's son.

Debashish suddenly burst out in laughter. Rajen-jyatha, indeed. No one ever called my father by that name. He was such a miser, everyone called him Miser Dasgupta. And that was reduced to Miser-babu. When we were young, even I used to identify myself as Miser-babu's son.

Trina remembered everything. The perennially ill have powerful memories. Everyone knew Miser-babu's son Debashish was a daredevil. You didn't see too many of such wicked, evil types. They weren't as young then as Debashish was making them out to be—the perpetually ailing Trina was thirteen, while Debashish was nineteen or twenty. He used to write love letters to all the girls in the neighbourhood— only the bedridden Trina was spared because he didn't take her seriously. Meeting that same girl after so many years, this time within the framework of a complete and fulfilled home and family, had left him more than a little astonished.

I remember women's faces clearly, he said. I wouldn't have recognized you otherwise. I still can't believe you're alive.

Probably thanks to Sachin's karma. Marriages are made in heaven. If you hadn't been alive Sachin-babu would have remained a bachelor even today.

It had all started innocuously enough. Indec was renovating their house, redecorating it, constructing balconies, putting windows in—Debashish would turn up once or twice a week to supervise the work. He moved at lightning speed from one spot to another, like a person with loads of work to finish. Serious, conscious of his position, Debashish wouldn't look anywhere else. Sometimes, after the supervision was over, he'd come up to Trina and say goodbye. Some days he would say, in a voice light enough to indicate the distance between them, Can I get a cup of tea, Kadambini?

He'd borrowed the name from 'Dead or Alive', Tagore's famous short story—Through her death, Kadambini proved she hadn't died. Quoting the line one day, Debashish had said, You are the person who's alive to prove she hasn't died, but I don't know, I still find it hard to believe.

In response, Trina quoted Eliot—I am Lazarus, come from the dead, come to tell you all, I shall tell you all . . .

Sachin wasn't home all the time. Reba and Manu were busy with themselves, like all children of rich fathers. Trina was by herself all day. She played a bit of carrom, a bit of table tennis, painted a little, wrote poetry. But none of this could be her companion. Instead, by sitting down with a book of poetry she could immerse herself in something distant.

Debashish was a well-known artist, director of two flop movies, very deeply connected with the world of intellectuals. That was what surprised Trina. How did that flippant, girl-chasing, precocious young man acquire all these qualities?

Sometimes, over tea or coffee, Debashish said, Do you really have something to tell, Trina?

What on earth would I have to tell? Trina asked in surprise.

You keep saying, I shall tell you all.

Oh! That's just a quote.

When people use quotes they have a subconscious motive.

I haven't any.

Debashish would be lost in thought.

Trina had invited Debashish and his wife to dinner on Reba's birthday. Debashish's wife came with him. His wife befitted him. Good figure, tall. Dark complexion, pleasant features. But all she could talk about was money, jewellery, their house and their car. She was dim-witted, or else she'd have realized that she was flaunting her wealth in a house whose inhabitants were a hundred times richer. Those who became rich suddenly didn't know what to do with their money—they scoured the markets like starving people and bought everything in sight, turning their homes into jungles. Old money didn't make such a spectacle of wealth, didn't show it off. Blinded by money, Debashish's wife couldn't see anyone but herself. Short of purring like a cat, her eyes glazed, she kept ticking off her husband. There were many guests that night. Trina hadn't been able to spend much time with them. The little interaction that she did have made her feel rather embarrassed. Debashish's wife was aware of nothing but the materialistic world and her own joys and sorrows.

All this had happened a couple of years ago. The renovation had just been completed. The all-new house glittered. Trina hadn't done up her room much. She didn't care for over-decorated rooms. That disturbed the greyness of her heart. She preferred simple, soft colours and airy, well-lit rooms. She liked melancholia, loneliness, poetry.

Trina, Indec couldn't build anything for you except a balcony, Debashish had said.

There was nothing for Indec to do for me. I don't like decorated interiors.

I know. You're hopeless as a client.

Trina had just smiled.

But unique as a woman, the rakish Debashish Dasgupta had said. It would have been wonderful if we'd met at the right age and the right time.

Oh, said Trina, feeling scared.

You've seen my wife, haven't you? said Debashish, putting on a sad expression.

I have.

Well?

Beautiful.

Who wants to know whether she's beautiful?

What, then?

Her nature.

How would I know? I saw her just once, we didn't talk much either. But she didn't seem rude or anything.

Only money and status hold any meaning for her, she has no sensibilities.

So what! All women are like that.

But you aren't!

Never mind me, Trina said sadly. I'm a little abnormal after having been ill so long. I think too much, I remain silent and distracted, I write poetry—all this is the result of my abnormal mind. That's why no one in this house likes me. Even my children tease me, calling me their intellectual mother.

Perhaps.

Listen, don't speak badly of your wife to others. It's not in good taste. Adjust to whatever you've got. You're too restless, too impatient, you used to write to too many girls. How do you manage to disengage so easily? You like people too easily, dislike them too easily too. You'll keep *chasing* all your life if your heart cannot settle down somewhere.

How did you know all this? Debashish laughed softly. I haven't spoken badly of my wife to you yet. I'd barely begun. You went and said a lot of things.

Trina was extremely embarrassed. She was far too imaginative. The moment anything happened, she would habitually work out a web of causes behind it. Once she had lost a bunch of keys to the cupboard and drawers. This happened a day after a servant had been sacked. Unable to find the keys in their usual place, she immediately assumed the dismissed servant had stolen the keys on his way out. Now he would put together a group of people from his village and turn up at the house. They'd murder Trina and rob the house. She had painted this imaginary scenario so vividly that Sachin had been compelled to inform the police. Even the police in the servant's village had been alerted. But on the third day, Trina herself discovered the keys in the niche in the bathroom wall for the soap.

That was how her mind worked. She had almost needlessly accused Debashish of bad-mouthing his wife, needlessly expressed a mild apprehension that Debashish had fallen in love with her. Embarrassed, she said, I just think there's something the matter with you. That you're not happy in your everyday life.

That's true, Debashish sighed. But there's nothing to be scared of.

But whatever he said, it was not all that safe. It was obvious Debashish did not love his wife. And Sachin did not love Trina. Or, that is what Trina's imaginative mind assumed. It was not untrue that Trina was quite happy to assume that Sachin did not love her, that Reba did not love her, that Manu did not love her. That no one in the world loved her. That she was alone, miserable. Whether that sadness had any basis or not, she liked to think that that was how she was. This sadness was what gave her a kind of romantic pleasure. The thought of sadness, or the sadness of thought, is very delicious for some people.

Debashish got wind of that. Just as he had identified all the damaged, broken and weak spots in the house and repaired them, so too did he easily spot Trina's specific vulnerability. But he didn't repair it, he only weakened it further.

Trina's heart had wanted something like this—an accident, a slip, a little sin, a little guilt that marked out life in the brightest colour. Picking out that vulnerability of hers like a flower, Debashish placed it in his buttonhole like a red rose. But why was the rose red? Trina had thought about it. It was red because shame was red. Some sins are black, some are red.

Trina put on the red sari. She dressed herself. It wasn't all that late, there was still time, never mind. Trina would walk around a bit. Then wait at the bus stop.

three

———————

S topping the car at the petrol pump, Debashish got out, stretched and yawned. Still yawning, he said, Twenty litres, and handed over a credit card from his pocket.

Robi had got off too, going up to the ice-cream stall. It's shut, Baba, he cried.

What to do?

Why is it shut? Robi came running, his boots thudding on the ground.

It opens a little later in the day. Let me buy you some candy instead.

Champa called out from the car, I've brought food for you, sweetheart, don't eat all this junk.

Standing in front of his father, Robi surveyed him through slanted eyes—tall, dressed in a shirt and trousers, a black-and-white silk scarf around his neck. A little distracted, his father tapped his toe on the ground, his hands in his pockets, a frown on his face.

Robi took his stance like a boxer—right foot forward, right

31

fist shielding his face, left arm stretched out. Taking a step forward, he punched his father in the stomach with his left fist, saying, Wham!

Debashish bent over double, stepping sideways. Then he turned around too, taking an identical stance to Robi's and landing a fake punch on his son's face. Swaying away quickly, Robi moved forward. Silently they shadow-boxed, their eyes on each other. Champa looked on from the car with smiling eyes. As he topped up the tank with petrol, the attendant laughed loudly.

A punch on his stomach made Debashish sink to the ground, doubled up. Throwing his chest out, Robi started the countdown like a referee—Ten, nine, eight . . . three, two, one, knock-out! He raised his finger heavenward.

Debashish stood up. Holding his hand out, he said, Congratulations on becoming the new heavyweight boxing champion of the world!

Thanks. The boy shook his hand, smiling. Then he said softly, May I make a phone call?

To whom?

My friend Ranjan.

Go ahead.

With firm, confident steps, Robi pushed the glass door open to enter the pump-owner's office, picking up the phone with practised hands. Debashish went closer to the office. He could hear Robi say, Hello, is Ranjan around? Yes, Ranjan, this is Robi . . . We're out for fun . . . First to the zoo, then to Monima's at Maniktala . . . Yes. Oh no, not Maheshtala, Maniktala . . . M for . . . M for . . .

Meerut, prompted Debashish from the door.

Glancing at Debashish out of the corner of his eye, Robi shook his head. M for mother, he said into the phone. A for . . .

Allahabad.

Allahabad, echoed Robi. And N for New Delhi, I for India.

Debashish retreated slowly, opening the door of his car and sitting down inside. He lit a cigarette absent-mindedly. The words rang in his ears. M for mother.

When Robi came back to the car, Debashish looked a little grim. Driving, he said—Why were you spelling that way? When you spell out a word on the phone it's best to use the names of places. Is mother a place?

Robi smiled like a baby. Of course it is, he said.

A place? What kind of place is mother?

Motherland, for instance.

Smiling, Debashish said, But you only said mother, not motherland.

Covering his eyes in embarrassment, Robi smiled. I made a mistake, he said.

Debashish sighed deeply. Robi had not forgotten, only hidden his feelings. Maybe he missed his mother very much. Who could tell?

Robi was kneeling on the seat, sucking his thumb, swaying with the movement of the car. Be careful, sweetheart, said Champa cautiously.

You're so scared all the time, said Robi, swaying at will. Can I go to the back seat, Baba, to Didi? he asked.

Yes, said Debashish, still distracted.

Champa reached out to collect Robi from the front seat. This was what he always did—alternate between the front and the back seats. He was very naughty. Debashish didn't scold him at all. He didn't have the heart to. Did the boy miss his mother very much?

Debashish had chosen Chandana as his bride. There was a time when he had relationships with several girls. He didn't know which of them he was ultimately going to marry. Chandana was the boldest and the most scheming of the lot. She became pregnant with Debashish's child even before marrying him. Debashish did not have the guts to abandon her at that stage. Chandana had not agreed to an abortion, saying, If you don't want to marry me, don't! I'll have my baby as an unwed mother.

That was her scheme. Debashish married her when she was two months pregnant. Robi was born as expected. Chandana was alive till he turned four.

She had a bad temper, and never considered the consequences of her actions.

His relationship with Trina hadn't deepened yet. Trina

used to call him over sometimes to discuss the ins and outs of art. It was an obsession with her at the time. She was frustrated at the smudging and at her own hasty brush-strokes when trying to paint her watercolours. Debashish had taught her how to wield the paintbrush. He made her practise mixing two shades to get a third. But she would take a long time over it, not realizing that the busy Debashish was wasting the time he normally used to earn money. She enjoyed it.

It wasn't as though Trina was very beautiful. Moreover, she was married, and the mother of two grown-up children. It was rather unusual for Debashish to be attracted to such a woman. He had met plenty of women, after all. What, then, was the reason behind this weakness for Trina?

There was just one reason: his adolescence. Memories from that time are very dangerous. Whatever else she may have lacked, she was enveloped in the scent of his memories. He had long forgotten that slight, sad young girl. But ever-turbulent time had brought her back to him anew.

Another reason was Chandana herself.

Why would Debashish want to destroy Trina's happy family? He had never been morally upright. But he did have taste. Indisputably, he enjoyed women when he got the opportunity. But he never lost his head over any of them. Nor was Trina a woman to lose one's head over. Although she wasn't past the age, she was still a mother and a wife. Was this any age for romance? Under the veneer of painting, though, they had heard each other's sighs of disappointment. One's was over Sachin, the other's, over Chandana. But then, it was also true that no one in this world belonged to another.

Had he not spent a large part of his life womanizing, Debashish might have acquired the ability to rein himself in. Or, had Chandana been the perfect wife, she would have reined him in.

That didn't happen. Chandana wouldn't leave him alone at home. She'd keep saying, I know everything, where you go to paint. Go to hell!

They'd moved into their nice flat by then. They used the lift, not the stairs. There was a car in the garage. Robi prattled continuously. They were taking shape as a family.

One morning, on a holiday, Chandana overslept. Robi had been poking his sleeping mother continuously. As soon as she awoke, she gave him a few slaps. When she hit him, she did it heartlessly, without any tenderness. Although a few minutes later she'd hug and kiss him effusively. Chandana was definitely eccentric.

But that morning onwards, something went wrong with Chandana.

Debashish was in the drawing room, just as usual, with *The Statesman* open, his feet on a stool, a cup of coffee next to it. Chandana grabbed the newspaper from his hands. What do you think you're doing? she asked.

What am I doing? a tired Debashish replied.

Others get punished for their sins. Why don't you?

Debashish recalled picking up his cigarettes and matches. Silently, he had prayed—Oh God, why is Chandana alive? What he said was—Shut up.

Chandana did not shut up. She flew into a rage, calling him names and hurling accusations. Eventually she burst into tears, babbling through them, You've cheated my father, you've cheated my son, you save money secretly . . .

None of this was true. It didn't make any sense, either. The doctor was sent for. He diagnosed a nervous breakdown, thanks to a cocktail of headache pills, sleeping pills, her own prescribed pills, worry, anxiety, etcetera.

Chandana never quite recovered from the trauma of the nervous breakdown. One day she killed herself, jumping from the sixth floor. It was very early in the morning. Robi and Debashish were still asleep.

Debashish, of course, was released by the court. But in her death Chandana came back into his life in a much bigger way than when she was alive. It was to forget her that Debashish deliberately stoked his thirst for Trina. What could be more intoxicating than what's forbidden?

Baba, Robi called.

Hmm, Debashish answered distractedly.

Why're we going to the zoo?

Don't you want to?

I've been so many times. I don't like it.

Where do you want to go, then? asked Debashish in surprise.

Nowhere, said Robi shyly.

Well then?

Let's go to Monima's house.

I see, said Debashish. Stopping the car, he smiled. Then he nodded, saying, Of course. The zoo can't be fun every day.

Let's go back.

Shaking his head, Debashish said, Didn't you say you wanted to eat at some Park Street restaurant? Don't you want to?

Smiling his clever smile, Robi said, Peiping.

Nodding knowingly, Debashish said, Don't you want to go?

I will. I want to take something for Buro-da, Ninku, Poltu, Thapi, Jhumu and Nani. I'd promised them a treat from Peiping this Sunday.

Is that so?

Yes, Robi smiled.

Debashish looked at him affectionately. He changed direction.

Baba.

Hmm.

Monima loves me so much.

I know.

Buro-da, Ninku, Poltu, all of them do.

Is that so?

Yes. So much. They never want me to go. They say, stay with us.

I see.

Why don't I stay with them, Baba? Monima loves me more than anyone else.

Debashish stopped smiling. At first, he felt incapable of speech. Robi looked at his father's face in silence for a long time. He probably realized from the expression that his father wasn't happy.

Champa said from the back, Whom will we live with if you're not at home, sweetheart? Baba hates it without you.

Let me stay with them for a few days, Robi answered.

You'll come back after that? Champa asked.

Yes. I don't like it without him either.

Debashish let the car fly through the Maidan. M for mother—he just couldn't forget that. He had deliberately locked away all of Chandana's photographs so that Robi didn't find them. It was very painful for a motherless child of that age to be reminded of his mother. Debashish had removed everything that had anything to do with her—her saris and other clothes, her cosmetics, her papers. He had distributed the saris here and there, giving some of the more expensive ones to his sister Phuli in Maniktala. She hadn't wanted them but he had insisted—They'll just rot, you must wear them.

One day, Phuli had forgotten and appeared in Robi's presence in one of Chandana's Jaipur-print saris. Gaping at it for a while, Robi had said in a strange voice mingled with tears and laughter, Monima, Ma had an identical sari.

It was very difficult to keep track of what went on in children's minds. When he realized how far back their memories went, how sharply and accurately photographic those recollections were, Debashish had experienced a strange kind of agony. Robi avoided mentioning his mother to him at all costs. He knew his father wasn't pleased if he did. That was how sensitive his childlike mind was.

Debashish experienced a wrench in his heart. Suddenly he felt a pang of love for his son. Seated inside a well-known Park Street restaurant, he pushed the menu towards Robi, saying, Order whatever you want, absolutely anything.

He looked at his son.

Robi looked back at his father in surprise. Blinking, he said, But I'm not hungry.

Really? said Debashish in disappointment.

Robi shook his head. Didi made me eat so much in the morning. Lifting his T-shirt, he pointed towards his stomach, saying, See how stuffed I am.

Chandana used to check several times a day whether Robi had fever or not. She'd place the back of her hand against his forehead, and then place it against her own for comparison. Sometimes she'd call Debashish and say, Let me check whether your skin is warmer or cooler than Robi's.

All mothers have these obsessions. His mother did, too. Moreover, Chandana would continuously harangue Robi to eat, and then check whether his stomach seemed full. If he didn't want to eat, she'd start with coaxing and cajoling him, and end with a few slaps. You'll starve to death,' she used to say. 'Do you think anyone will worry about your meals after I die?

Whenever she asked him to eat, little Robi would display his stomach to his mother.

Lowering his T-shirt, Robi said with entreating eyes, I can't eat, Baba.

All right, said Debashish with a sigh.

Baba.

Hmm.

Monima doesn't touch chicken.

Debashish remembered. You're right. But I've gone and ordered it.

What'll we take for her then?

What do you think we should?

Sweets, Baba, okay?

All right.

Robi smiled happily. Debashish always did as Robi asked. Things happened according to his wishes. It wasn't like that when Chandana was alive. She used to be furious whenever he demanded anything. She scolded him, spanked him. And yet Robi used to follow her all over the place. Swallowing the scolding and the spanking, he'd stick to her like a leech.

What *was* so attractive about that bad-tempered, stupid woman? Debashish couldn't figure it out. Nobody in her family was happy with the circumstances in which they had got married. Chandana's father had actually beaten her black-and-blue and trussed her up in a room. Her mother had cried herself into hysterics. In that troubled situation, it had no longer been possible to ensure that the marriage took place in an atmosphere of civility. Debashish laid siege to their home one day, along with a few friends. The local young men had been bought off already with fat donations for the neighbourhood Durga Puja. Debashish left with a threat to Chandana's father—If you beat her again, expect serious trouble.

Chandana's father was scared. To be decent was to be a coward. The castigation stopped, but her family still didn't talk to her. Debashish used to rent a room at his sister's house those days. His brother-in-law had not approved of his marrying a pregnant woman and bringing her home. His sister didn't like it either. Chandana telephoned frequently, saying, I'm not asking for much, let's just go to Kalighat and you can put a little sindoor in my hair. That's all.

No way, Debashish would say. I'm going to have a full-fledged wedding with you and bring you home.

He'd done just that. Turning the city upside down, he'd found a house in Jadavpur to rent. He was not short of money. With lots of jewellery and saris thrown in, he organized a flashy wedding. A cousin of Chandana's represented the bride's family.

Debashish found it strange that he had gone to so much trouble for a woman as worthless as Chandana. Shortly after the wedding, she prodded him into buying an expensive flat—with unobstructed views to the south and the east—in a swank neighbourhood. This huge enterprise had been in vain. Shortly after the wedding, Debashish realized there was nothing heavenly about marriage. Chandana wasn't fit to be his wife. How could he live with someone so shallow, bad-tempered, impatient and wealth-obsessed? Despite his immoral ways, he had a certain artistic detachment, some little business integrity and work ethics. He believed that when the man returned home after a day's hard work his wife should provide him shelter like the shade of a tree on a scorching day. The wife should be a place of rest.

Most days, Chandana wasn't home when Debashish returned. She'd be out shopping, or at the cinema, or at her parents' house. After the marriage, Chandana's relationship with her family had somehow improved dramatically. That was the time Trina became intimate with him, like a boat on a single, isolated current. A sharp current, but secure. Debashish had never fallen in love with anyone. Now he had. An unbearable situation. An impossible love.

There Robi was, sitting across the table from him now. He felt like asking Robi how he now thought of Chandana. Why did he love that bad-tempered, worthless, shallow mother of his so deeply? He wanted to ask Robi that. He wanted to know if there was a way, somehow, for him to have loved her.

The waiter brought a huge packet, wrapped in brown paper, on a tray, along with the bill. Paying the bill and adding a tip, Debashish got up. He glanced at his watch. Plenty of time to go. The time that would have been spent at the zoo had been saved.

f o u r

No matter how much she dressed up, Trina's face never lost its forlorn appearance. A desolate, unhappy, arid expression was permanently stamped on her guilt-touched features. Her eyes held a frightened restlessness.

As she was leaving, Manu rushed in through the gate on his cycle—a fabulous red sports cycle. He was dressed in white shorts, a white sports-shirt and sports shoes, with a red Turkish towel over his shoulders. His arms and legs were beautifully proportioned, his chest broad. He was carrying a tennis racket. Placing one foot on the ground, he stopped in the portico. Lifting his eyes, he glanced quickly at his mother.

Trina almost melted into the heavy glass door. She felt her heart jump. The moment their eyes met, she seemed to lose all strength in her limbs. Manu seldom spoke to her nowadays, ignored her for days on end.

Trina couldn't move an inch from her spot near the glass door. Still sitting on his cycle, Manu used his foot to lower the stand. Leaning the cycle against it, he climbed upstairs on light feet. He gave Trina another fleeting glance. Manu looked older than his fourteen years. Not only was he large for his age, but his eyes were also mature beyond their years—something he had probably inherited from his father. His father too was more severe in temperament than his age warranted, his behaviour more like that of older people.

There was a large coir mat at the door. Balancing against the doorframe, Manu scraped his shoes on the mat. The smell of perspiration, of sunlight, wafted into Trina's nostrils. Who would believe that she was the mother of this smart, grown-up boy? Their appearances were dissimilar, their behaviour was dissimilar, and on top of that Manu hardly bothered about her any more. How long it had been since Trina had heard someone call her Ma.

Seeing her shrinking against the glass door, Manu took another look at her, frowning. He seemed to sniff something in the air. Suddenly, he said in a very casual voice, Chanel No. 5, isn't it?

Trina was startled. He was right. The perfume she had had someone send to her recently was indeed Chanel No. 5. But she was so taken aback that she couldn't respond. Transfixed, she stared at her son with her large eyes, as though possessed. Her spine gave way these days when she tried to look her son in the eye.

Not that Manu was waiting for her reaction. He ran inside, crossing the lobby and bounding up the stairs. He would now take a cold shower, change and go out.

Trina stared unblinkingly at the direction in which he had vanished. She couldn't leave straightaway. She walked around slowly, crossing a big stretch before taking the stairs to the first floor. She'd rest a bit before going out.

Manu and Reba had their rooms at the southern end of the house. She now stood in the middle of the hall, hearing soft whistling from one of their rooms. One step at a time, she went towards their rooms. She never visited this part of the house these days. Her children would be annoyed if she did, frowning, or getting out of her way. In this family, she was on one side, while her husband and children were on the other. Invisible arrows were fired from their eyes, weapons of silence were hurled at one another.

Manu was in his room. The door was ajar, the curtains hanging behind it. On the other side was Reba's room. It was silent. Trina stood outside the door, listening closely. No, there was no sound inside. Summoning a huge reserve of courage, she pushed the curtain aside with weak, trembling, cold hands, and stepped inside. The room was empty. On one side stood bookshelves, a desk, a wardrobe, a cupboard, while a few expensive chairs were arranged in the middle. There were fresh flowers on the low centre-table. There was a faint scent of incense everywhere.

Reba was only twelve, but her lifestyle was that of an adult woman's. Trina sat for a few moments on the bed with the foam-rubber mattress. Fear claimed her heart. A framed photograph of Reba's stood on the desk. She was slim, with a thin, arrogant nose and oval eyes. Everything added up to a stamp of sharp intelligence. Manu looked a little duller in comparison—he was nowhere near as intelligent as Reba was. Reba came first in her class at Modern High School. She was on course for a high statewide rank in the final school examinations. Manu wasn't as sharp; all he wanted was to be the India No. 1 at table tennis or some other sport. A friendly, good-tempered boy, he had a transparent personality. That was probably why he still spoke to his mother once or twice.

But Reba's gravity was solid and uncompromising. Her manner of ignoring Trina was as sharp as her intelligence. Reba humiliated and scorned her mother in as many different ways as possible. It was rare for a girl to be so hostile towards her mother. No matter how much Trina feared Manu or Sachin, she feared Reba a hundred times more. Women's eyes saw everything, their minds took in everything. Trina considered that slightly built girl in a frock the most fearsome person in her life.

The room smelled of incense, of cosmetics, of room-freshener. The walls were light blue and grey, the ones facing each other were the same colour. There were different kinds of light fittings, curtains on the windows and door, china dolls lined up on the pelmet. A radio receiver and a cassette player were arranged on the bookcase, while the music system and the cassette-shelves were next to it. The interior decoration of the entire house was Debashish's. All the furniture had been supplied by his company.

Trina looked in trepidation at Reba's photograph on the desk. She felt as though she was actually sitting opposite Reba. That Reba was looking at her. Reba's lovely smile in the photograph seemed to be changing to one of derision and hatred.

A tear-laden sigh emerged from Trina's quaking heart. Just like the scent of distant rain, the tears gathered together in the air. Trina could smell them. But in vain. She had shed many a tear, though no one had bothered.

It had been a long time since Trina had visited this portion of the house. Having stolen in now, she was rather enjoying it. At twelve, daughters become friends with their mothers. So much excited girl-talk is exchanged at this stage. The daughter remains a daughter no more, becoming a confidante instead.

But alas, Trina and Reba would never be friends. Reba, sharp and cruel as she was, would push the cowardly Trina to the edge of her sanity.

Trina rose. Reba was at her singing class. She would return soon, but she wouldn't return silently. Her quick, running footsteps could always be heard a long way off. So Trina was emboldened to walk around Reba's room, to leaf through her books, to run her hands over her dresses, skirts, trousers and saris in the cupboard. A nightdress lay on the bed. Sheer, imported fabric. Folding it, she put it away. She straightened the bedclothes. The desk was already neat. Still, she moved things around a little, discovering a few drawing notebooks, filled with watercolours. Trina's heart knocked against her ribcage. Did Reba paint!

Trina discovered paintboxes and brushes on top of the bookcase. Yes, beyond doubt, Reba did paint. On a low shelf by the door were arranged Reba's tabla, harmonium and tanpura. She even found a book of poetry on the harmonium case. A surge of joy fluttered in her breast, like a newborn bird. Did Reba read poetry!

Trina opened the bookcase again. The books weren't arranged properly, so it was difficult. But still, a little search yielded quite a few books of poetry. In surprise, she started flipping through them, losing track of time.

Preoccupied, she didn't hear the footsteps till it was too late.

Reba stopped short as soon as she entered. Her lean, sharp face suddenly became suspicious, distorted. Frowning, she threw a look at her mother before kicking off her sandals, sending them flying into a corner. Like a whirlwind she spun around to stand before her mirror. She had looked at her mother with what seemed to be a mixture of surprise and loathing. The rest of her behaviour radiated indifference.

She wore a contemporary-styled orange dress. Although she was thin, Reba was quite tall. Once she put on some weight, she would have quite a good figure. Standing in front of the mirror, she pressed a spot on her face, then rubbed the area with her finger.

What have you come to tell me? she said.

Trina started. She remembered she was a trespasser in this room. Disaster was imminent now, she could no longer run away from it. Softly, she asked, Classes ended early today?

This is the time they end, replied Reba in irritation. What do you mean, early?

She continued scanning her face in the mirror, possibly looking at Trina's reflection once or twice. But Trina didn't dare look that way. Staring at the floor like a criminal, she said, Do you paint, Rebu?

Reba was perhaps a little surprised. Yes, I do.

I didn't know.

They teach us drawing at school. Everyone knows.

Do you read poetry?

I do.

Trina sighed.

Anything else? Reba asked aggressively.

Nothing.

I have lots to do. I need to change. Leave, please.

I'm going. Trina stood up. At no age was a girl embarrassed about changing her clothes in her mother's presence. Still, Trina stood up defensively. Unable to drum up an important enough excuse to be in the room, she said weakly, I came to see what new music you have.

Without answering, Reba continued to look into the mirror.

Trina said in a subdued voice, I saw saris in your wardrobe. Do you wear them?

When I want to. Go now.

I'm going. I have a lot of saris. Want some?

No.

Why?

I have plenty. If I need more, Bapi will buy me more.

Exhaling, Trina nodded with a frown. She knew this. If necessary Sachin would buy Reba every sari in the market. Reba could choose them herself, too. Still, it was a tradition in Bengali families for adolescent girls to dress in their mothers' saris. This didn't stem from a paucity of clothes. The mother dressed her daughter in her own sari and smiled to herself. Mothers were reborn in their daughters in that way. But Reba didn't need that.

Trina felt her mouth turning dry. Her hands and feet were chilled, her head was bursting, her breath, fiery. She took a couple of steps towards the door, then turned briefly. Her brows were furrowed, dry tears in her eyes. How easily this chit of a girl could decimate Trina's motherhood.

The family was split down the middle. Trina on one side, Sachin, Manu and Reba on the other. A syndicate. Miles of disparity lay between the rooms all day. No one was on her side. But even so, did Manu feel a pang for his mother sometimes? Trina had wondered about this a lot, but never managed to come to a conclusion. Once in a blue moon, Manu would address her as Ma. Maybe even say a few words to her. Maybe ask for something at the dinner table. Trina was quick to pass whatever he wanted. If Manu wanted something done, she complied obediently. But even with so much yearning in her heart, Trina knew that in truth Manu felt no special bond with her. He was a simple boy, all he thought of was sports. He didn't remember to loathe his mother continuously. He forgot, distracted by other things. Just like when he said a short while ago, smiling, Chanel No. 5, right?

Reba didn't forget. She nurtured unending indifference and hatred within her like a snake. She was never distracted from it. She was only twelve, she probably hadn't even had her periods yet. But how she still withheld everything from her mother. How independent she was—how fearless.

Despite her assurances of leaving, Trina waited, saying, I have heaps of jewellery in my locker. I'll send them to you, you can use them.

Who asked for them?

Why should you have to ask? They're yours by right.

I don't use jewellery. That too gold jewellery. God! Reba made a horrible face.

Trina emitted a repulsively needy laugh. That's true, she said. Girls of your age don't like solid gold jewellery. You can have them remade.

I don't want to. You can wear them.

You're such a little girl, how many *can* you put on when you're so thin? I have lots. I'll have plenty left over—they're all yours anyway.

Nothing of yours is mine. If you don't want them, give them away.

Why? Why isn't it yours?

That's how I like it. I get a headache at all this talk of clothes and jewellery. Go now.

Wrong weapon. But this wasn't exactly a case of Trina luring her daughter. This was more to do with Trina using random conversation as a ploy to extend her time in Reba's room, for she knew Reba lacked for nothing. Girls these days didn't go weak at the knees at the thought of clothes and jewellery.

Reba sat at the other end of the bed, swinging her legs. The bell on her silver toe-ring tinkled. Her pose was one of relaxed indifference. At this age, Trina had spent all her time in bed. She didn't have such a fresh, adult demeanour. All she had was apprehension, doubt, low self-esteem. And yet Trina was, in a sense, happy at what she saw. She felt her daughter would take after her. She painted, read poetry, wasn't addicted to clothes or jewellery.

Manu could be heard singing tunelessly from his bathroom, accompanied by the sound of gushing water. The sound of the water made Trina thirsty. Her heart had turned to stone, really. The thought of a drink of water hadn't even occurred to her.

Like a beggar, she said, Can you give me a glass of water, Rebu?

Reba was very annoyed. The mask had come off her lean, intelligent face—it was easy to see the anger, the irritation, the petulance on it. Her eyebrows, nose, eyes all shrank into a frown. Still, she rose, pressing a switch like a piano key on the wall next to her desk.

Somewhere within the house, a bell rang out two musical notes. The maid appeared in silence.

A glass of water, said Reba.

This was how it was supposed to be. Trina knew, of course she knew, that Reba wouldn't pour her a glass of water herself.

The maid brought chilled water from the cooler in the hall. A transparent cut-glass tumbler placed on a tray, with a crystal cover. The water glittered like a diamond. Trina drank all of it.

Done? said Reba. Go now. I'm getting late.

Are you going out now? It's so hot, said Trina like an obedient girl.

What if I do?

Where are you going?

I have things to do.

I don't have all the books of poetry you've bought. Will you give me some of them? I'd like to read them.

Without answering, Reba proceeded to pull out the clothes she wanted from her wardrobe, laying out a long skirt and a blouse on the bed. A light purple skirt of pure silk. A golden blouse with needlework.

How lovely!

What do you mean, lovely? Reba snapped.

The outfit. When did you get it?

Raising her slim, sharp face, Reba observed Trina deliberately, for more than a moment. Trina looked away.

Just go wherever you were going, said Reba.

Trina still spoke with beggarly greed, It's very sunny today, aren't you taking an umbrella?

That's my business.

Rebu, I'm not feeling well at all.

Go lie down in your room.

Why're you behaving this way?

Without responding, Reba walked into the attached bathroom, slamming the door.

Trina stood by herself in the empty room. She really wasn't feeling well. Rather unwell, in fact, as though a fever was coming on. Her eyes smarted, her limbs were no longer under her control. And in the realm of her mind, she sensed chaos. She simply couldn't arrange her thoughts in any kind of order.

Trembling, Trina left with very slow steps. The hall was dark and cool. She stood for a while, then numbly let herself fall into the soft couch set against the wall, right next to the indoor plant placed in the huge painted wooden planter. The leaves of the plant brushed against her cheek.

Trina sat there in a daze for some time. She hadn't looked after her health in ages—who knew what diseases had taken root within her? She couldn't think coherently. Her memory stumbled; disjointed thoughts swam up in her mind. She wanted to sleep.

She raised her face at the sound of high-pitched whistling. Dressed in a white T-shirt and blue jeans, Manu was on his way from his room to the staircase. Pausing a moment, he glanced at the watch set into the bracelet dangling from his wrist. He looked like he couldn't believe what he saw. Not noticing Trina, he continued on his way.

Hidden behind the leaves, Trina looked at her handsome son. He already knew how to drive and play tennis, and had even learned western dance. He inhabited a world far removed from Trina's. She couldn't believe that this healthy boy had actually emerged from her womb. Even if she did believe it, she swayed between extreme pride and extreme fear. But it was true that in Manu's world, there was no one named Trina.

Manu reached the head of the stairs. He would disappear any moment.

Trina couldn't get any vigour into her voice. Faintly, she said—Manu.

By rights, Manu shouldn't have been able to hear her. He was at the other end of the huge hall, whistling a popular song and perhaps even preoccupied with adolescent thoughts, along with the joyous attraction of the world outside. He shouldn't have been able to hear his mother's faint cry. Still, after taking a couple of quick steps down the stairs, he stopped. And looked around. Maybe he had a faint suspicion that someone had called.

Here, Manu, said Trina in the same faint voice, from behind the leaves.

This time he heard and looked back with a slightly stupefied expression. No matter how grown-up he looked, boys of his age were still dependent on their mothers.

Manu spotted her from a distance. Trina was dressed in a flaming red sari. She had worn an expensive foreign perfume, and had used make-up. The dress of a wanton woman. Was that why Manu had joked, Chanel No. 5, right? when he entered the house? Was wantonness writ large all over her?

Manu climbed back up the steps, crossing the hall with giant strides to come up to her. A very annoying and mocking smile played on his face. Lightly, he said, That's strange, I thought I saw you go out.

Trina lifted her parched face towards him. How large, how enormous these people were.

I didn't go, she shook her head.

So I see. What's the matter?

Where are you going?

Out.

I'm not feeling well at all.

Did a hint of anxiety, as fleeting as a ripple of water, play across Manu's face? Lie down if you're not feeling well, he said.

His face was exactly like Trina's. He took after his mother. His eyes held a feminine softness. All this came from Trina. He had many of her physical traits. Noticing this after a long time, Trina sighed deeply.

Leaning towards her for a closer look, Manu said, You've dressed up, haven't you? But you're looking pale. Your eyes are red too. Go lie down in your room.

Will you help me to my room?

Come, said Manu, extending his hand.

Trina was astonished. Was he going to touch her? Wouldn't he be repelled? You aren't getting late, are you? she asked timidly.

What if I am? Let me take you to your room.

Trina was about to get up. But stunning her, Manu picked her up suddenly, and with a laugh said loudly, Gosh, how light you are!

Trina felt dizzy, unable to breathe. Let me go, she moaned.

You think I can't carry you all the way?

You'll drop me, she said faintly.

Rubbish! Don't you know I'm a weightlifter? You're as light as a bird, he said, rocking her as she lay in his arms. Trina inhaled her son's fragrance. A subtle scent of soap, powder and insect-repellant pellets from the wardrobe. And, piercing through all of this, couldn't she also sense Manu's flesh-and-blood smell, a certain rhythm in his body?

Manu crossed the hall without difficulty, cradling Trina. She had her eyes closed in fear, her hands clutching his T-shirt.

Placing her on her soft bed, Manu said, Saw that?

Smiling a little, Trina said, Don't admire yourself so much. You'll jinx yourself.

Everyone else does. They call me Samson.

God forbid.

Manu smiled lightly, foolishly. I'm off.

Where are you going?

Lots of places to go to.

Manu jerked his head. Raising his hand in a salute from the door, he left.

The scent of her son still remained with her. Manu had always been a plump, heavy child. She had found it difficult to take him in her lap. Everyone used to comment on his health. Now he had a body to boast of. Naturally, everyone stared. Trina felt happy at the thought. But the regret was that her son was hers but not hers. Sometimes, out of sheer forgetfulness, maybe he thought of his mother as his mother. And then stepped back immediately. Everyone became distant again. And Trina shrank in fear. She had so many different fears. In silence, she kept thinking of Manu.

Sachin had gone somewhere, but he was back now. His tuneless humming in the next room became audible again. The clock chimed in the hall. Trina listened to it from her room, still in a daze. But as she listened, she was startled into alertness. Eleven o'clock!

Her heart beat faster. Not in excitement. Sitting up suddenly had done it. The bus stop wasn't very far away. Debashish would be waiting. Trina had become far too old among her own. To live in this world she needed someone with whom she would be born afresh every day.

She got up. She wasn't feeling well—physically or mentally. Even if she went out now in the middle of the day, and didn't return for a long time, no one would be anxious. No one would worry for her.

A raised voice was heard in the hall. Bapi!

Hmm, answered Sachin.

I'm going out.

All right.

Sachin had succeeded in chaining all the birds to their rods. No one in this family felt as defeated as Trina. Sachin was both father and mother to the children. Trina had no idea where they went, or what they did. For instance, she didn't know which of them would have lunch at home that day and which of them had lunch invitations elsewhere. No one told her anything. They only told Sachin. Alone, angry at her deprivation, Trina pouted. Standing before the mirror, she smoothened out the creases in her sari. She would go out now.

On her way out, she saw Sachin bent over the plants, inspecting them. He had his back to Trina. He was a little over forty. Healthy. Yet, she could see that his posture held traces of old age. He looked like a mature, thinking, decisive person, the signs of an experienced head of a family written all over him.

Trina had come out of her room in silence. Sachin shouldn't have been able to sense her presence. Yet he did. Suddenly bending to pick something up, he turned to look at her. He held a small hanky. Trina's.

Is this yours? Sachin asked.

Made of a very fine fabric and lace, it was hers all right. She must have dropped it while seated on the sofa.

Trina nodded.

It was lying here next to this plant. Putting the hanky lightly on the sofa, Sachin went back to inspecting his plants. Trina had heard he was getting bonsai plants from Japan. They would be put in glass cases in the hall. He was probably making plans.

Trina had to go very close to Sachin to retrieve her hanky. She had to practically enter the environment of his breathing, his smell, his body-heat. Trina sensed an electric current within her body. Sachin, however, was distracted. He didn't even notice her.

Picking up her hanky, Trina was about to go towards the staircase, when she stopped. She wasn't afraid of losing anything; she wasn't hopeful of gaining anything, either. So why not test this man too, after Reba and Manu? Sachin had hit her some time ago. That must have been the only time in his life he had stumbled. He probably hadn't felt any emotion for Trina at any other time. Why was that assault of his a happy memory for her!

Suddenly Trina said, I'm going.

Sachin didn't hear her.

Desperate, Trina said, Hey!

Still distracted, Sachin answered, Hmmmmm?

Then he turned to look at her. His eyes were completely absorbed in some other thought.

I'm going out, said Trina breathlessly.

Sachin seemed very surprised. He looked at her flame-coloured sari and make-up, wide-eyed. Much later, he said, Oh.

Sachin was low on passion, low on anger. But he was always severely dutiful. Surely he had some reaction to the fact that his wife had taken an immoral path, but expressing them was not his practice. In fact, he had not thrown her out although he could have. Instead, he had given her wonderful comforts. He didn't even care for public opinion. What kind of man was he? It could be that he didn't love Trina, had never loved her. But whether or not he loved her, shouldn't a man be possessive at the very least? Or have self-respect? Trina wasn't feeling well today, her thoughts weren't coherent either. Otherwise she would never have dared to do what she did. She knew perfectly well Sachin wasn't concerned about her. He didn't keep track of her whereabouts.

With incredible effort, Trina looked Sachin in the eye.

Sachin was extremely grim. He was distracted no more. He looked a little worried.

Nodding, he said, Go, then. What's to say?

This was the answer Trina had been expecting. But today something desperate was working within her. She kept thinking that she needed to know the truth behind these relationships, taut with anxiety and trepidation. She felt as though there wasn't much time left.

So Trina said, There's nothing more you have to say?

What else is there to say? said Sachin in surprise. The stage of saying anything has passed.

Trina bit her dry lips. Her mouth felt parched, her tongue as coarse as a doormat. But amazingly, after a long time she didn't feel any fear, nor did her heart quake, as she stood before Sachin.

If I were to go away once and for all? Even then you wouldn't have anything to say? asked Trina.

I'd have plenty to say. But I wouldn't want to say anything.

Why?

To speak is to make someone listen, I don't have anyone like that.

Trina was silent. Tears came, but she did not cry. What value did her tears have anyway?

Sachin picked up the jug from the table and took a swig of water. Then, looking at Trina, he asked in a concerned tone, Are you leaving once and for all?

Trina didn't say anything. She only looked on boldly.

Sachin said, You could have taken this decision much earlier.

What purpose would that have served?

At least the anxiety and tension could have been avoided. Debashish would have been relieved, too.

I wasn't talking of that kind of going, said Trina impatiently.

What, then?

I don't think I'll live much longer.

I see. Sachin was silent for a while. Then he nodded, as though he had understood. He said, That's possible, too. Your nerves have been under severe stress for quite some time. On top of that, there's the complex arising from continuous guilt. Many people would want to die in such situations.

Are you trying to be sympathetic?

No. But I'm urging you to be courageous. Why do you want to live like a thief? Whatever you have done, you should have done with more courage and decisiveness.

Explain. Explain clearly.

Sachin looked at her for a while, as though he couldn't quite believe Trina was behaving this way. Then he said, This isn't the place to talk. Come this way.

Sachin went into the room at the front end of the hall. The room had a green table-tennis board, a carrom board and a chessboard. On the wall were arranged tennis and badminton rackets. A golf set lay in a wooden frame. There was a shoe rack to one side. Guns and rifles were hung in a wall-mounted cupboard, while a few comfortable sofas lined the walls.

Trina couldn't quite believe, either, that Sachin would show any keenness to talk to her. The whole thing seemed to be happening in a dream. But Trina knew that talking was not going to solve this problem.

The room was a little dark. Sachin waited for Trina to come in, and then shut the door. There were some very bright lights in this room to play table tennis by. Sachin switched them on. Dazzlingly bright lights.

Trina was feeling perverse. Inside that room with the door closed, she thought Sachin had called her in there to stage some happy-ending drama. He wouldn't put his arms around her or something, would he? No, Trina wouldn't be able to stomach that. It would be far too distasteful for her.

Pulling up a chair to the table-tennis board, Sachin leant on it carefully with his arms and looked at Trina. All right, tell me now.

What should I say? frowned Trina.

It was you who started it.

Trina was startled into silence.

Time was running out. Debashish would be waiting in his car at the Ballygunge bus stop. As soon as she thought of that, a wave of sharp, intense joy washed away her physical weakness. When she looked at Sachin, she felt reluctant to be in his company.

Sighing, Trina said, I will probably not live much longer.

Why do you say that now, suddenly?

I'm saying it now because it occurred to me now.

Shaking his head, Sachin said calmly, Even if you do feel that way, what can we do about it?

I didn't ask anyone to do anything, said Trina impatiently.

What, then?

Trina reflected. The words didn't fall into place in her mind. Suddenly she said, Don't you know what my life is like in this house?

Sachin looked at her in silence. Maybe he applauded this show of courage in his mind.

Then he said, I know what it's like from the outside. But how do I know what it's like within you? Every individual is actually two persons.

How's that?

The person we see performs all the actions, maintains relationships, laughs and cries, loves and hates. And the person within is a lunatic. He has no resemblance with the external person, no compatibility; at best a compromise. No one except a real god can get to know that person within.

I'm not interested in your theories.

Sachin looked calm and at ease. Trina could never accept this tranquility of his. Sachin now said calmly, Theories don't necessarily come out of books. Theories and philosophy all come from life. I am telling you very clearly that there's nothing more we can do for you.

I know. But still, there's something I want to know. What do you think of me now?

Sachin didn't smile. But an indecipherable amusement still twinkled in his eyes. Apparently, you're still quite beautiful, he said. You have a great figure, you don't look like the mother of two children.

Trina went red with anger. That's not what I asked, she said.

What, then?

I want to know what you think of me.

Oh. Sachin went on looking at her in silence. His eyes held no words either, besides a silent amusement. Actually, I don't think of you at all, he said. I've had to work hard to get into this habit of not thinking of you.

Trina knew all this. Still, she said, But here I am in front of you. Still no reaction?

There is.

Like what?

We don't notice beggars on the road. But when one of them becomes bold or desperate enough to come and tell us their story, we feel bad for them. We feel pity. It's the same thing— I feel bad for you, pity for you. When that beggar mingles with the crowd again, we won't notice him any more. None of us can remember anyone else constantly, no matter how much we love them or hate them. They come to mind, we forget, they come to mind again . . . That's how relationships go on. People exist in two ways for others.

How do you mean?

One, just physically. Two, in their minds. For me, you exist only physically, not in my mind.

Trina frowned. Not in irritation—frowning was her normal response to feeling helpless.

Exhaling, she said, That isn't true.

Then what's the truth? Do you exist in my mind?

I didn't say that, Trina shook her head. I wanted to know . . . What's your reaction to me?

Sachin bent his head and looked at his fingers splayed on the green table-tennis board. Without raising his head, he said, I'm very sympathetic. I understand your problem, which is why I was asking you to be courageous.

Are you asking me to leave?

Shaking his head, Sachin said, No, you can do whatever you want to even without leaving this house. You well understand it makes no difference to us, but it does make a difference to you. You're suffering from guilt all the time, you suspect us of speculating about you. Perhaps you even think that Debashish's wife killed herself because of you. All this is eating away at you. I'm not asking you to leave, but that would be best for you.

Doesn't it make any difference to all of you whether I stay or go?

No.

And if I die?

That's different. When we see others die we think of our own death, so we feel depressed. But why should you die?

I didn't say I would die out of choice. But I don't think I will live much longer.

That would be sad. You should do something so that you don't have to die. Go to a doctor if you're not well.

Trina walked to the door. Stretching her hand out to unlock it, she said, I will. But please do not imagine I was talking of dying to earn your—or anyone else's—pity.

Sachin pushed his chair back to get up. He didn't say anything.

Trina didn't look back any more. Opening the door, she went out into the hall. Then she climbed down the stairs and took the garden path out to the pavement. She walked very quickly.

Why shouldn't I leave? I'm not part of your family, she muttered to herself.

Since she didn't have a destination in mind, she found herself on the wrong road. There wasn't much time left. Debashish would come. They would meet at the bus stop near Ballygunge. As soon as they met, the dead colours of the world would be tinged with brightness.

Trina decided she would tell Debashish today that she would go to him for good.

Just down the road, a young man was kick-starting a motorcycle. He kept jumping and pressing down on the starter with his foot. The bike refused to start, roaring once or twice before lapsing into silence. On that silent road, the sound and its echo became louder and louder. It seemed to jolt Trina back to her senses. She looked around her to realize she was on the wrong road. The Ballygunge bus stop was further north.

She turned around and walked on. Behind her the motorcycle finally roared into life and came charging at her with a horrific sound. Trina jumped on to the pavement. Raising a thunderous din, the motorcycle crossed her and went on its way.

f i v e

As soon as she heard the car, Phuli ran downstairs, panting. She had become rather fat at an early age. Mother of a bunch of children—and yet her fondness for children had not abated. Her love for Robi knew no bounds.

Phuli's display of love was old-fashioned. Robi was barely out of the car when Phuli drew him into her arms, still on the road. Moaning with happiness, she kept saying, My precious! My angel! My beautiful! as she rubbed her face on his chest and face. Embarrassed at first, Robi tried to stop her with his arms and legs, but he had his weak spot too. He waited avidly all week for this unsophisticated demonstration of love.

As they went up the stairs, Robi already had his arms around her, his head on her shoulder. I dream of you every night, Monima, he said.

These words set off a fresh wave within Phuli. She crushed Robi against herself, still moaning with happiness. And Robi soaked it all up shamelessly.

Hearing them, Phuli's children surrounded Robi, shrieking. He was a huge source of wonder to them. He spoke English as well as a foreigner; he was dressed in extraordinary, expensive clothes; and he followed social protocol flawlessly. Phuli's children found all this extremely entertaining.

Releasing Robi among her children, Phuli kept looking at him with besotted eyes. He's lost weight, she said to herself.

Putting down the boxes of food and the containers of sweets, Champa said, He doesn't want to eat anything.

How can he eat? Phuli shook her head. He's burning up inside. I know.

They didn't have a separate drawing room. The entrance led into a longish corridor of sorts, with a few chairs. Phuli's husband Sisir worked in the Railways. He wasn't very old, but extremely conservative. As they seemed to have children every year, Debashish had once told him, You'll kill your wife, and the children won't be looked after properly, either.

Cocking his head, Sisir asked, So what do you suggest?

Why don't you use contraceptives? Debashish asked.

Sisir was furious. Why, do I go to whores? Why do I need to use all that?

That was Sisir for you. He had no clue about the modern world. He was convinced that the moon-landing was nothing but a hoax for publicity. He still didn't believe man had really set foot on the moon. If the subject came up, he just said hmmm like an expert and busied himself with other things.

He simply could not tolerate Debashish. Maybe he envied his financial success, or disliked his modern, fashionable ways and his clever conversation.

Debashish sat on a chair in the corridor for a few minutes. His cousins had surrounded Robi inside with noisy celebrations. The chicken had probably emerged from its box. Phuli's children were roaring in delight. Sisir appeared from the direction of the bathroom, a cheap local towel round his waist. He smiled at Debashish. How are you? It wasn't a very convincing smile.

All right.

Is Robi here?

Yes, can't you hear him?

Sisir finally had a real smile on his face. However much he might dislike Debashish, he had a soft spot for Robi. When Robi came, Sisir bought him sweets, toffees, toys. He called him Robiraj.

Phuli brought Debashish a cup of tea, covering her head decorously when she saw Sisir. She had acquired the air of a matronly housewife, paan in mouth.

Putting the cup of tea on a small stool, she panted—I made halwa, will you have some?

No.

Paying a quick visit to the bathroom to spit out the paan, Phuli returned. Looking at Champa, she said, Are you staying all day, Champa, or going back with Dada? I can't manage by myself any more on days like these. The little hooligans ransack the house without any help, and today their father, the devil himself, is home too. Why don't you spend the day here?

Champa nodded. I don't like being away from the boy anyway, she said.

Phuli's face radiated happiness. Poor boy's lost weight, she said.

Out of politeness, Debashish sipped his tea. In truth, he hated the tea that Phuli served. Instead of flavour, all it had was the liqueur and a mass of milk and sugar. There was too much milk in it now, turning his tea white. As children, they used to call this foreign tea, obviously because of the complexion of foreigners.

Phuli, this is foreign tea you've give me, Debashish said.

Phuli didn't understand at first. When she did, she said, Everything about you is very international. Do you suppose we can remember all that about light liqueur and very little milk and sugar? I just made it the way we make it in Bengali families. Let me make you another cup.

Don't bother. It's not bad, said Debashish.

Phuli drew up a stool to sit on. With the jewellery she had on and the key she carried around her waist, she made a jangling sound whenever she moved. She breathed laboriously, punctuating her breaths with ohs and ahs that signified pain. She probably had some feminine malady. Although she kept complaining of various ailments, she never stayed in bed. She worked hard all day, like a steamroller.

Dada, you have to take a decision about Robi, said Phuli as she sat down.

About what?

What's the use of forcing him to stay in that haunted, empty flat? All kinds of phobias tear him apart all day. Can't you see how he's losing weight? Doesn't want to eat, mopes all day. No friends either.

He'll get used to it.

I don't see him getting used to it. He talks about his mother with me quite often. When I make him take a nap in the afternoon, he jerks in his sleep all the time. These are not good signs. He's too shy to say anything, but deep within he cries.

Debashish was distracted. Putting his cup down, he said, But I give him whatever he wants.

Bah! The biggest thing for children are their mother and their friends. He has neither. I'll tell you what, let him stay with me. Don't you see how he dotes on his Monima?

Debashish smiled. You already have a few, if you add Robi on top of that . . .

Don't say such things, Phuli ticked him off. There's no such thing as too many children.

So you aren't through with wanting children, Debashish said.

No, said Phuli sternly. And I never will be. There can never be too many children. The more I have, the more I want. What am I a mother for?

Although there was no logic in this, you couldn't protest

against it either. For this was something much stronger than logic. This was faith. Living with Sisir had probably instilled all these crude notions within her. It would be stupid to fight faith with logic. So Debashish remained silent. He lit a cigarette.

Let's see, he said.

There's nothing to see. Let Robi stay with me. I beg of you.

His school is close to that house. Besides, he's become used to a particular lifestyle. If he stays here he won't be able to settle down.

What rubbish! Have you ever seen him want to leave when he's here?

That's when he's here for one or two days. The trouble will start if he has to move in permanently.

That's my problem. You're too obsessed with turning your son into an Englishman or an American. He uses English even with me these days—throws around thank yous and sorrys.

Sisir had changed out of his towel into pyjamas. Coming out of his room, he said, He doesn't want his son to grow up in a poor family. He won't learn good habits here. His food and drink won't be scientific either.

That was precisely what Debashish thought. Living with the mob, Robi would forget his polished manners, his smartness. He would learn to scream, to use profanities. And, perhaps, he would gradually forget Debashish.

No, it's not that, he said softly. It's only because of him that I even want to get back to the flat.

But how long do you stay? said Phuli. As soon as the night is out, so are you. He just goes back to his lonely existence.

Let me think about it, said Debashish with a sigh.

I'll look after him with all my heart. You needn't worry a bit.

I know that. But let me think it over.

Don't crush him while you think it over. If he stays here he will forget everything. It's because he stays in an empty house that his memories haunt him. He tells me so much.

Debashish looked at Phuli disbelievingly. How boundless her desire for children was. She didn't think of the labour pains or the trouble afterwards. She was still upset because of two miscarriages. Deprivation, poverty, bad times—all of them had accepted defeat to her. She probably never even bothered to read the government proclamations about having no more than two or three children. If you told her, she would say that even listening to all this is a sin.

Honestly, said Debashish with a smile.

Will you give me Robi? asked Phuli like a beggar.

Looking away, Debashish said, I need to go now.

He got up. Champa ran to Robi. Come along sweetheart. Your father's leaving, say bye to him.

But Robi didn't come willingly. Debashish waited near the stairs. Champa finally led Robi to him by the hand. His hair was already dishevelled, T-shirt rolled up to his chest. He was blissfully happy, as his expression revealed. As soon as he saw Debashish from a distance, Robi shouted, Go now, Baba!

All right. Debashish gave him a tortured smile.

Phuli came with him up to the stairs, climbing down a few steps with him. Listen, Dada, she said in a low tone.

Hmm, said Debashish distractedly.

It won't be good for Robi to stay with you. He's miserable. Why don't you understand?

Debashish smiled. Like a corpse. He descended to the road, leaving Phuli behind.

As he opened the car door, he looked up suddenly on hearing a voice. He was shocked out of his wits. Robi was leaning over the first-floor railing, half his body hanging in mid-air. His cousins clustered around him. They were looking at something in the distance in great excitement, pointing it out to one another. Maybe a kite. Or a helicopter.

Debashish felt a jolt in his heart, like a car that brakes suddenly.

Robi! he screamed loudly.

The scream was a big mistake. You should never call out to anyone in this situation. Robi's mother had jumped to her death from the sixth floor.

Half his body suspended in mid-air, Robi was startled on hearing his name. His tiny body swayed. Reaching out blindly for support, he balled his hand into a fist helplessly. A few lethal, teetering moments collapsed together. Debashish's almost unconscious body slumped against his car. He shut his eyes. Gnashed his teeth.

Robi regained his balance. His cousins had dragged him backwards. They were pulling him off the railing. Phuli stood behind them.

Debashish stared incredulously. Robi smiled at his father through the railing. Then, suddenly, he pulled his toy revolver out of the pocket of his shorts, aimed at his father and fired. Bang! Bang! Bang!

Debashish considered returning to Phuli's house. Then he thought, no. She had children too. None of them had ever fallen to their death.

Debashish smiled at Robi too. The make-believe bullet from Robi's toy revolver seemed to have hit him somewhere in his chest. Somehow, through the open door, he collapsed into the seat behind the steering, and then took several deep breaths.

He began driving. But all he could see through the windscreen was the sight of Robi leaning over the railing. He started again and again, grinding his teeth. His knuckles whitened at the force with which he gripped the steering wheel. He drove, making mistakes all the way.

He simply couldn't forget that Robi's mother Chandana had jumped from the sixth floor.

Had Robi not forgotten anything either? He remembered everything.

He was going to meet Trina. At the Ballygunge bus stop. Debashish began driving very cautiously.

Trina was walking faster down the deserted afternoon road. Someone was following her. She looked back—nobody was there. But she kept thinking someone was following her. Secretly. Someone's eyes were keeping her under strict surveillance, like a detective. No one. Yet Trina walked as fast as she could. The main road was ablaze with cunning sunlight. All the shops were closed. The roads were deserted. Was she going to be murdered today? Did some assassin keep chasing her from the shadows?

Trina looked around her. Nobody. She had gone a long way in the opposite direction. The bus stop was still quite some distance away. Trina couldn't walk much. Walking was a very exhausting affair. She never took rickshaws either. She felt far too compassionate. On these melting roads, in the afternoon heat, under this whiplash glare of the sun, those emaciated people pulling their vehicles along—Trina simply couldn't bear to be their passenger.

A taxi was parked by the petrol pump at the Landsdowne

Road crossing. The driver was reading a small book, his legs drawn up. Probably a form book—or it could be the Bhagavad Gita. Trina never took a taxi alone. She was far too scared to. But the deserted road made her tremble even more. She was afraid. Paranoid.

Gathering her courage, Trina took a couple of steps forward.

Taxi? Will you go?

I will, dead-panned the driver.

The taxi was parked facing southwards. As soon as Trina got in, it continued in the same direction. Trina hadn't said anything yet. She could vividly see herself sitting in Reba's room, and the heartless Reba looking at her with cold, transparent eyes. The very next moment she could see her son—the strongly built, big-boned Manu was taking her to her room in his arms. How fresh and reassuring he smelt. Then she could see Sachin sitting across the table-tennis board, saying, I don't think of you these days . . .

Trina frowned. She was no longer part of her own household. Nobody noticed her. What was this? She was someone's mother, someone's housekeeper. Her steep fall, this calumny, this extra-marital love—why didn't any of this make them agitated or sad? Was their peace of mind, their everyday behaviour, so unaffected? Was this Sachin's conspiracy? Had Sachin instructed them?—Don't look at her, don't talk to her, ignore her. There was no greater punishment.

The middle-aged driver—he looked like a brute—kept looking at her through the rear-view mirror. It was a small mirror—only his cruel eyes were visible in it. Trina was startled when her glance fell on them suddenly. A sound of terror leapt into her throat. Clamping her hand over her mouth to prevent the sound from escaping, she said, Stop!

You want to get off here? asked the taxi driver, slowing down.

Right here, said Trina, surprised to see she had arrived at Deshapriya Park. She wasn't supposed to be here, she had to be at the Ballygunge bus stop. Why then did she keep drifting away from that spot repeatedly, absent-mindedly and mistakenly? Where are we? asked Trina softly. Is this Deshapriya Park?

Yes, is this where you want to get off? said the driver, this time turning his head to look at her squarely. He was perspiring, boorishness written all over. Trina sensed an animal lust in him. She trembled a little. In her hurry, she couldn't even unlock the door. Briefly she wondered whether he had slyly fixed the door so that she couldn't open it. He suddenly pushed her hand aside with his own perspiring one and unlocked the door.

Trina was about to rush away. She was in a big hurry. The

taxi driver called out sarcastically from behind her, And who'll pay the fare?

How you make mistakes when you're in a hurry and scared. Trina opened her bag and paid him. Her face and ears burned in embarrassment.

To quickly escape the taxi driver's line of sight, Trina paced around aimlessly for a while, walking up to Rashbehari Avenue. She simply couldn't recall which bus would take her to Ballygunge. She felt very restless, a constant fluttering of wings in her breast. The parrot's cry kept haunting her, Trina . . . Trina . . . Trina . . .

That afternoon, Calcutta could easily be called Solitary City. There was no one to be seen anywhere. A desolate, unhappy street, the sunlight cascading everywhere. Trina had to go to the Ballygunge bus stop, but it seemed to be a very long way off, a distance that could not be bridged—perhaps ever. It was past one in the afternoon. The scent of Trina's Chanel No. 5 dwindled away slowly, the wind making her hair fly all over the place.

Standing on the pavement of Rashbehari Avenue, Trina bit her lips, thinking. How would she get there? She was supposed to have been there at noon! As she pondered, Trina looked back again with unease. Who was it that was following her? Who was observing her intently?

Terrified, Trina suddenly saw a No. 42 taking the turn.

She realized that this bus would take her to the Ballygunge bus stop. Racing like a deer, she crossed the road ahead of the bus. Stop, stop please! she shouted as though besieged.

These buses were ready to stop anywhere for passengers. This one did, too. Trina boarded with difficulty, for it was crowded.

Debashish hadn't become successful without reason. He had some unusual qualities. One of them was patience. As soon as she got off the bus, Trina saw Debashish's car waiting at the bus stop. A constant stream of cigarette-smoke emerged through the window.

An exhausted Trina approached the car, patting her hair into place. She smiled wanly.

But Debashish remained unsmiling. Get in, he said, opening the door. Plopping down in the seat, Trina said, You must have been waiting a long time. I got really late.

Just the opposite, said Debashish, shaking his head.

What do you mean?

It was I who was late. I arrived just a couple of minutes before you did. I was convinced you must have gone back. I was about to leave too, when I suddenly saw you getting off the bus. Why are you late?

Exhaling, Trina shut her eyes and said, Lots of things happened just as I was about to leave. I was in Reba's room, while she wasn't there. When she came back, she behaved very badly. Then I had an argument with Sachin. I was so put off, so distracted, that I took the wrong way and went off in a different direction. Why are you late?

Same story, said Debashish, as he drove. As I was about to leave after dropping Robi at Phuli's, I saw him at the first-floor railing . . . Visualising the scene again, Debashish shuddered once more. He continued softly, Phuli wants to take Robi away. Robi doesn't care much for my company either.

Trina was silent. Trying to suppress a sigh, she felt her insides caving in. After a long time, she said, Have you decided to let Robi stay with her?

I didn't want him to. But he probably will. I was very distracted when I left. Skipped two red lights, the police took down the car number. Hit an old man at Park Circus, though he didn't die. After driving madly like that for some time, I realized it wouldn't be right to continue driving. I drove slowly to the office, had it unlocked and sat quietly in my room. I wasn't feeling normal. Lost all sense of time. Why do you suppose Robi doesn't care for me any more? I give him whatever he wants. Why, then? Can you believe it, Trina? In that empty office even someone as unsentimental as me had tears in his eyes!

Drive slowly, you're very distracted. We're skidding all over the place.

Debashish brought the car under control. He said, I took the decision in the office. Then I took a taxi back to Phuli's place. I was in no state to drive. I told her, Phuli, Robi will stay with you from now on. How happy she was! You wouldn't know from the way she started jumping up and down how overweight she is. Robi was asleep, I didn't wake him. Just kissed his forehead and came away. My son now belongs to someone else. Oh well.

Trina was crying silently. All you could hear was the occasional sound of her heaving. Reaching out and touching her, Debashish said, Don't cry. We can't have everything, can we?

Without lifting her head, Trina spoke, her words punctuating her sobs, I've come away too. Forever. I won't go back.

Debashish looked grave. Calmly he said, Good thing, too. Didn't Sachin have anything to say?

He said lots of things. Plenty of philosophy. He advised me to come to you fearlessly.

Knitting his eyebrows, Debashish reflected on this development—Sachin thinks he's giving me a chance. I am ready for the catch, Trina. Sachin is out.

Trina hunched forward, sobbing.

Debashish let her cry. All he said was, Aren't you hungry, Trina? I am.

Trina didn't answer, only shook her head.

Her crying was irksome. A woman hunched forward in the passenger seat, weeping—it was quite a scene. Anyone outside could see it through the windows. Many had, too. Debashish was feeling a trifle uncomfortable. There was no food at home. He'd planned to eat at a restaurant. But given the state Trina was in, he ruled out going to a restaurant. They would have to go home, after all. And yet, how thirsty he had been for Trina till this morning. Wasn't he still? But all he could think of now was Robi. He had left Robi with Phuli. Had he got Trina in exchange for the rest of his life? Should he weigh them on a scale to find out?

He still couldn't get his head around the idea that Trina had come to him forever. That she was now within his reach. That they would live in the same flat from now on. Debashish had thought theirs was an impossible love. Two boats, two streams . . . So much more.

Trina was showering in the bathroom. Debashish waited outside. It was only four in the afternoon. Pritam had already brought them a cup of tea, and then gone out to buy something for them to eat. They'd eat as soon as Trina came out.

Lighting a cigarette, Debashish stood by the enormous window of his flat. The pavement was a long way below. This was that killer window. With what courage had Chandana leapt all that way down? He suddenly felt an urge.

Drawing the curtains apart, Debashish opened the window and leaned out. His head reeled. A yawning emptiness beckoned to him with open arms—come, come. On the sixth floor, a strong wind played all the time, in all seasons. How strong? The cool, soothing wind charged at him. Even in the face of that wind, however, beads of perspiration appeared on Debashish's face. How far away the pavement was! How strong the temptation of a headlong fall! The earth called everyone to its bosom, all the time. When Chandana abandoned the support of the window frame for the last time, how had she managed to traverse that long, gaping emptiness, into which her body plummeted? Hadn't she wanted to live again? Didn't she think of anyone? Did she cry? Had Chandana remained Chandana during that fall? He wanted to know very urgently. Debashish suspended his body, waist upwards, outside the window, and looked down. People crawled like insects, cars moved, there were one or two trees, black roads. How dreadful. His cigarette went out quickly in the wind. Debashish threw the stub down. After floating for a bit, it fell, taking a very long time—falling down . . . down . . . down . . .

He heard the bathroom door being opened. Trina came out.

Debashish hauled his body back inside. Tears pricked his eyes because of the wind.

Trina's tears and melancholy had been washed away by her bath. She looked solemn. Two single beds lay in the bedroom, made up for the night. Next to it was a covered area for changing. By the window was a long dressing table with a mirror at which Trina now sat. Chandana used to dress up here.

Trina looked at herself in the mirror. Her appearance did not require much attention. She worked on her face a little. Arranged her hair. She never used too many cosmetics.

Debashish's reflection appeared in the mirror. He was standing behind her. A small smile on his face, his hair all over the place.

How do you feel, Trina? he asked.

Fine, said Trina with a sad smile.

From now on . . . Debashish stopped. What could he say?

Trina finished his sentence in her mind. She lowered her eyes in embarrassment. Go, Deb, have your bath, she said.

Debashish showed her the cigarette between his fingers. In a minute, he said. As soon as I've finished this.

Go into the other room, then. I can't dress up in the presence of a man.

I see, said Debashish and went through the curtains. He spoke from the other side. Trina, listen, tell Pritam to get you whatever you need. Of course, it's Sunday, which means the shops are all closed.

What should I ask him to get? I don't need anything.

You haven't brought any clothes, have you?

Don't you have any saris of Chandana's?

No. Given them all away.

Why?

For Robi's sake. If I'd kept them, he'd have been reminded of his mother.

Trina had been fine all this time. But this was like a blow. Still, she smiled, saying, Isn't he reminded anyway?

He is. He keeps it hidden. I didn't do up this flat, you know. Chandana did. Nothing's been changed. I'd think of moving things around, but I never got the time, I've been very busy. Naturally he'll be reminded of Chandana. You can do it up now.

No, silly. That's not how you're reminded. You just don't know.

Debashish exhaled loudly. I needn't worry about Robi any more. He won't remember anything once he becomes part of the gaggle at Phuli's.

Are you done with the cigarette?

I am.

Go now. I'm very hungry.

You didn't tell me what you need.

Lots of things. I didn't bring anything. But there's no hurry.

Don't think twice before asking for something. This isn't a stranger's house—it's your own.

Really, said Trina with a sigh.

It isn't?

Is it so easy to make it your own? asked Trina with a smile. It takes a long time. Give me time, don't rush me.

Why? Why should it take a long time? asked Debashish from the other side of the curtain, the pique clear in his voice.

How can it not! When you uproot a tree, do you suppose all its roots come out at one go? So many pieces of the root, snapped threads, stay in the earth.

Trina . . .

Mmm?

The tree hasn't been uprooted at one go. Wasn't the earth around the roots being eroded for a long time?

I'll say it again, you're silly.

Why?

Can metaphors explain everything? There's a difference between a tree and a person, after all.

Parting the curtains, an agitated Debashish came into the room. Sitting down on the floor near Trina, he raised his face to her, saying, Trina, I'm so greedy.

Oh, I know.

I have no one to call my own.

Trina looked at him.

Don't frighten me like this any more. If you too have left your broken roots somewhere else, where do I go? Robi's not mine any more either.

Don't you understand how you feel in your heart about Robi? asked Trina tenderly.

Only too well.

Am I not allowed to feel that way too?

Debashish was silent. Taking out his packet of cigarettes from the pocket of his baggy shirt, he pulled one out and lit it. Then he nodded, I understand.

Trina continued in the same tender tone, We can't quite be like others, can we?

That's true, too, said Debashish. Then what will we be like, Trina?

We won't be very happy. There will be something keeping us a little apart.

You're speaking very plainly today, Trina.

It's best to say it today.

Why? Why today?

Wiping her eyes, Trina said with a smile, It's the day of rest. You have the time. Tomorrow onwards you'll be a busy man again. Will you have the time?

You're changing the subject, Trina.

Have your bath. I'm hungry.

Still Debashish sat there. Silently. After a long pause, he raised his face. Trina.

Tell me.

You can't sever a person from all their relationships. Not loving someone doesn't mean snapping all ties with them. And loving someone doesn't necessarily mean starting a new relationship. What'll we do with our love, then?

Trina pressed her forehead with her fingertips. Back to

93

philosophy. Don't you know women don't like philosophy? I have a headache, please have your bath quickly.

Pritam had laid out the food on the table. Expensive items from a well-known restaurant. Pritam was courteous, though he wasn't smiling.

When Debashish sat down at the dining table, Trina still had her forehead in her hands. Can you send your man for some pills? she said.

He's your servant, said Debashish said softly. But there's no need to send him—I'm sure there are some pills at home. I just have to find them.

I get a headache if I'm forced to stay hungry or if I cry.

With his eyes, Debashish signalled Pritam to leave. Then, taking Trina's hand, he said, I know you haven't come here prepared. You came on an impulse. That's why you're crying. But I've been prepared for you.

Very prepared indeed, smiled Trina. If you'd even kept one sari at home—I can't change out of this sari till I get a new one, even if that means waiting till tomorrow.'

Give me a day. Please. Everything will be all right tomorrow. The shops are closed today.

Trina nodded. Time! Time! Wait, there's this line of poetry about time . . .

She couldn't remember. Her head seemed to be bursting.

After you've eaten, you can rest. I'll draw the curtains, just lie down in the dark.

Where are you going?

Nowhere. I'll stay by you. Like a chatterbox.

Trina smiled affectionately.

It was almost five. The golden sunlight glinted on the sixth-floor windowpanes. Evening was still a long way off. Trina lay in the bedroom, the curtains drawn. Her body was tinged with the glow from the beige curtains. Her headache was retreating, thanks to two pills. She was overcome by the day's fatigue. But still she couldn't sleep. Debashish had stroked her forehead for a long time. Trina lay motionless, pretending to be asleep. Thinking she had fallen asleep, Debashish had gone out on tiptoe.

The room was not exactly dark. But it was not lit up either. A very safe haven on the sixth floor. Trina lay by herself. Her headache was gone. Exhausted, she reclined on the soft bed. This was a kind of lethargy. A pleasant lethargy. But she wouldn't get any sleep. Trina wouldn't get any sleep for many moons now.

Opening her eyes, she looked at the smooth paint on the ceiling, the square walls. There was a mysterious light on the walls. As she looked, she felt that same prickling sensation on her skin. Someone was observing her. Observing her very closely.

Trina started in surprise. Raising her head, she glanced all around, before putting her head back on the pillow and shutting her eyes. But she had the continuing sensation of being observed, of being observed relentlessly. Chandana's ghost? Or a projection of her own mind? Maybe it was herself. Wondering, she turned her head, her eyes opening of their own accord. And she screamed loudly, sitting upright, Who's there? Who is it?

The person standing on the other side of the curtains leading into the dining room now parted them, poking his head in. It's me, Pritam, he said in a heavy voice.

What do you want? asked Trina, looking at him suspiciously.

Sir asked me to tell you when you wake up that he's gone out. He'll be back soon, said Pritam, smiling nervously.

Where has he gone?

He didn't say. Took the car.

I see.

Trina's heart was still pounding. Pulling her loose sari tightly around herself, she got up. Wait, she said. Show me around the rooms, let me get familiar with them.

The servant didn't answer. He did not seem pleased either. He stood there with an expression of suppressed annoyance or loathing. Maybe he was under the impression that Debashish had picked up a streetwalker and installed her in the flat. Debashish had not informed him who Trina was, after all. Even if he did, Pritam would not understand. Who has ever understood the truth of the love betweentwo people in such a situation? Everyone makes their own assumptions.

There were two bedrooms. One dining room. One drawing room. A large, open, airy flat. The second bedroom was Robi's. It was packed with toys, a tricycle, picture books, a small wardrobe. Trina spent more time in that room. Make me a cup of coffee, she told the servant.

The phone rang in the drawing room. It kept ringing. The servant was in the kitchen. He wouldn't be able to hear it. Trina hesitated—should she answer the phone? The very next moment she decided the fear was unfounded. If she had to stay here, she'd better shake off these weaknesses. She went into the drawing room, answering the phone in a lazy voice, Hello.

A young voice was heard, Baba? Oh . . . The voice stopped. Then, stating the number, it asked whether it had reached that number.

Robi, realised Trina. She knew the number written on the phone by heart. Who is it? she said.

Who are you? said Robi, waiting. Then, suddenly, in a frightened voice, he asked, Ma?

Trina did not know how to answer this. She waited, the telephone pressed to her ears. Robi was telephoning. If Trina said it was the wrong number and put the phone down, he would telephone again. And not just that day, but also the next day. Perhaps he would need to talk to his father frequently. Where was Trina going to hide? And why should she hide? Still, she needed some time to digest this first encounter. Wrong number, she said, her eyes shut.

She put the receiver down, not able to understand why Robi had asked whether it was his mother.

Pritam brought the coffee. The phone rang again. Pritam looked at her. Tilting her head, she said, That's Robi on the phone. Don't tell him about me.

Pritam answered the phone. Hello, Robi-babu?

. . .

No, the phone didn't ring.

. . .

He's gone out.

. . .

No, I'm alone. Aren't you coming back?

. . .

Isn't Champa-di coming back? All right, I'll tell him. I'll send your things tomorrow.

. . .

But why won't you come back?

. . .

I'll tell him when he comes. Bye.

Disconnecting, Pritam left after looking at Trina out of the corner of his eye.

Five thirty. The doorbell rang.

Assuming it was Debashish, Trina got up to answer the door quickly, only to be taken aback. It was not Debashish, but a smartly dressed young man. He was taken aback as well. Isn't Debashish home? he asked.

No, he's gone out.

I see, he said, looking very curiously at Trina.

Should she ask him to come in?

Robi's not home either? he asked.

His eyes held a clear question—who are you? But he didn't ask, hobbled by decency. I'm Robi's uncle, he said.

Oh? Please come in.

What's the point? No one's home. But even as he said that he did come in. Hesitating, he sat down. Sighing, he rubbed his hands and said, You must be a relative of his.

Yes, Trina smiled gently.

Chandana was my sister.

Disentangling the knots in her hair, now falling loose, Trina said, I thought as much. Please wait a few minutes, he should be back soon.

Glancing at this watch, he said, I can wait a bit. I was thinking—he paused to organize his words—actually it's our marriage anniversary tomorrow. I was thinking, Debashish-da will come. Of course, if you'd also . . . Of course it's very sudden . . .

Trina felt a wave of sympathy for the young man. He couldn't size up the situation, though he was trying to. Have some coffee, she said. He'll be back any moment.

The young man kept staring at her with unseemly curiosity,

looking away whenever her eyes met his. But still he looked. Trina got up on the pretext of making the coffee. Informing Pritam in the kitchen, she went into the bedroom and sat down quietly. She could hear the man talking to Pritam. Low tones. This was how it would be from now on. It would take a long time for Trina's position to be determined. A long time. Trina sat there, ashen-faced, absent-mindedly untangling her hair.

It was past six by the time Debashish returned. The young man was still sitting in the drawing room. Debashish was carrying a few boxes of saris, flowers, some cosmetics, bags of food. Chandana's brother was surprised at the sight. Trina watched the scene through the curtains.

No, Debashish didn't panic. Smart people look very serious when caught in such situations. So did Debashish. They had a short conversation. The young man left.

Trina, Debashish called quite loudly.

What? Trina answered, not walking into the room but standing by the curtains.

I've got you all that you need, Debashish smiled broadly.

Where did you get all this?

While I was sitting at your bedside, I remembered that when I lived in Jadavpur, all the shops there would be open on Sundays. Take a look.

Trina rolled with laughter after she had scanned the provisions. What on earth have you brought?

Why?

Do you suppose I like such colourful saris?

You don't?

This is what Reba likes. And so many cosmetics! When have I ever used such ultra-modern lipstick, and all that kohl too?

Start now, Debashish smiled. When are you going to stop pretending to be an old woman?

My daughter's grown up, she'll probably start seeing boys soon. Who knows whether she isn't already?

That's the problem with Bengali women, Debashish smiled. Why won't you dress up, Trina?

Trina smiled too. A tender smile. Robi had telephoned, she said.

Debashish's smile died—What did he say?

I answered. I said it was a wrong number and disconnected. He telephoned again afterwards, Pritam answered.

Never mind, said Debashish, after some thought.

He rose and went away to change his clothes. He had another cup of tea.

Trina, he called.

Mmm.

How do we start?

What? What are you talking of?

Don't you understand?

No?

This life of ours.

What do you mean, start?

If it were a wedding, there would have been rituals, a wedding night. Even a registered marriage has its own chants. What shall we start with?

Embarrassed, Trina said, Don't say all that, it sounds very odd. Are we starting anything—have we even ended anything?

Is that what you think? The answer to that could be that you cannot start something unless you have ended something, Trina.

Philosophy again.

You're the one talking about the beginning as the ending.

Listen to me, Deb. I haven't ended anything, nor have I thought of starting anything. I've left my home, I was hounded out. I don't even know myself what I'm doing. Everything is mixed up. I cannot come to any conclusions today. There's just one thing I know.

What, Trina? Debashish leaned forward eagerly.

I need you very much at this moment. Nothing more.

Then we shall begin in that primitive way, Trina. When there were no rituals, only desire.

No! Please don't talk like that.

Debashish leaned back. I was a rogue when I was young. I used to pass love letters to girls. I used to drop a kite on Basanta-babu's terrace every day with the words I Love You written on them, addressed to his daughter Rani. Starting was no problem back then. I hadn't learnt to think, to construct, to organize—that was how I started. It began on an impulse with Chandana too. First it was physical, then an attempt to love, then frustration and the end. I can't start that way with you, after all. I have a big problem on my hands today.

There's no need to think so much today. Calm down.

Exhaling, Debashish said, It's a very strange day. Do you know? I left Robi at his aunt's place permanently. And then you said you were coming over. Didn't Sachin say anything?

What would he say?

He relinquished his right so easily? And what did you say before leaving?

What would I say? Trina frowned. I didn't say anything.

Debashish was startled. You haven't said anything?

No. I left, just like any other day.

Doesn't anybody know you're here?

No.

Haven't you told anyone?

No.

Silly.

Why?

If you don't go back they'll inform the police, check with the hospitals!

They will! You think so!

Won't they?

I don't think so. Do they even know I exist?

Very silly of you, Trina. You should have told them. Would Sachin have bitten you?

It's not that. They haven't worried about me for ages. Let them worry a little tonight.

That isn't right, Debashish shook his head.

He rose and started dialling the phone. Going up to him, Trina said, Don't telephone. Let me remain lost for some time. Let them fret.

That isn't right, Debashish shook his head. Busy, he said, listening to the sound from the other end.

Trina sighed in relief.

Debashish turned around—Whatever I do will be permanent. Without uncertainties, without doubts.

It was not quite quarter to seven yet, but almost. The view through the sixth-floor windowpanes showed the enormous expanse of Calcutta's sky. Stars twinkled in the firmament. The city could be seen stretching out a long way, radiant with lights.

The drawing room was dark. Or, not exactly dark—a zero-power bulb glowed under a coloured glass cover. The curtains were drawn. There was a moon outside. A square, white patch of moonlight lay inside the room. And wind, like a storm.

Debashish sat by himself, like a spectre. He was dressed to go out. His legs were stretched out before him, his head resting on the back of the sofa, his face staring at the ceiling. His hands were splayed helplessly at his side. He was thinking of Trina. Borne along on cross-currents, a mad wind in their sails, heading in opposite directions, the two boats had still managed to dock with each other. Nice.

Trina was getting ready in the other room. They were going out. Trina didn't want to. She wasn't feeling well today.

Debashish said, Going out makes things better. You have a problem with roots, after all.

Trina didn't like going out. Her favourite pastime was being by herself in a corner of her room where she could paint, write poetry, read, or listen to music. Conversation annoyed her. Long periods of illness in childhood had accustomed her to this solitude.

The phone was ringing. Debashish stretched out his hand to answer it.

Hello.

A female voice said, Is Debashish Dasgupta there?

Speaking.

Oh, Dada . . .

Phuli. Her voice sounded odd on the phone. Debashish was extremely frightened. His body became numb as though stunned by an electric current. Was Robi all right?

Phuli! What is it?

You're back! Thank goodness. Robi has been going on and on about you for a long time. He telephoned twice.

What's happened?

Nothing. Why should anything have happened? Don't fret so much. Robi is with me, and I'm the mother of several children.

Tell me what it is? said Debashish, irritably.

Robi wants to talk to you. He's been asking why you were late getting home.

Is he upset?

Not at all. He's at his naughty best. Enjoying himself.

Give him the phone.

In a minute Robi's voice could be heard. Baba.

Yes. Debashish's voice became tender.

We're out.

Where?

We've taken a taxi. Now in Shyambazar.

Who else is with you?

Monima, Pishemoshai, Ninku . . .

Enjoy yourself.

Baba, when are you sending my clothes and books and toys?

I'll send them with Pritam tomorrow.

Can I go to school and still stay here?

You can.

And Didi will stay with me, won't she, Baba? I can't have my meals unless she tells me a story. Monima said that Champa can stay.

Let her.

You aren't angry, are you, Baba?

Angry? No, why should I be angry?

Because I came away to live with Monima?

Why should I be angry because of that?

You can't live without me, that's why.

Sighing, Debashish said, I can. I have to.

Ninku was saying—Your father will be scared without you. Is our house haunted, Baba?

Haunted? Who's been telling you about all this? No such thing.

Thapi was saying.

What was Thapi saying?

Robi seemed embarrassed. When people die, they come back as ghosts to haunt you, Baba. So . . .

So what?

Thapi said it. Not me.

What did Thapi say?

Thapi said that after dying, Ma has remained in the house, as a ghost.

All that is rubbish, Robi. You're not to believe any of it.

Buro-da also said, Don't go back home Robi. If you do, your mother will kill you for sure. Ghosts always kill the ones they love so that they can take them away.

Really, Robi. If you're going to start saying and believing all this I'm not going to let you stay there.

Didi tells me all these ghost stories, too.

I'll tell Champa not to. You don't have to listen to those stories.

All right. But Baba . . .

Tell me. Debashish sounded grim.

When I telephoned in the afternoon . . .

What?

I thought Ma answered the phone.

What on earth are you saying?

No, it was a wrong number. But I was very scared when I heard the voice of the lady who answered. I was sure Ma's ghost was answering the phone.

It isn't right to imagine such things. Don't do it any more.

Baba, I won't go to school tomorrow.

Why?

I haven't brought my uniform or my books.

After a little thought, Debashish said, All right, you can start the day after. I'll write a note, so that you can take the school bus over there.

Tomorrow's a holiday then, Baba?

Holiday.

Where shall we go then tomorrow?

Where?

Robi laughed into the phone. Such a pleasant, amused laugh. Monima says we're going to your flat tomorrow.

Worried, Debashish said—What's the point? I won't be here.

Monima says she'll take me herself, pack all my things, and do up the flat, too.

No, there's no need.

We shouldn't come?

Why bother, Robi? I'll send your things.

Wait then, let me tell Monima.

Debashish could clearly visualize Robi discussing things with Phuli, covering the mouthpiece with his hand. He felt very worried. And in that short interval, he concluded that his luck with women wasn't good. The first time around, he had married Chandana, complete with a child in her womb. The second time, the woman he was bringing home would have to be torn away from her grown-up children, her husband, her home. He just couldn't have a simple, straightforward relationship. As though he was committing a sin, surreptitiously.

Hello, said Robi.

Yes.

We're not coming tomorrow.

All right.

We'll come on Sunday.

I'll visit you on Sunday, Debashish laughed.

Then when?

What do you mean, when, Robi?

When will I visit our flat?

Whenever you want to. Why call it a visit—this is your own flat. Come any time you want to. Not this week, that's all.

Then we'll take a taxi to Dakshineshwar tomorrow.

Do.

All right, Baba. Good night.

Night.

Debashish disconnected. His brows were knitted with worry.

A beam of light entered the dark room from the doorway. Trina stood, still as a statue, with that light behind her.

Debashish groaned softly in pain, though he didn't know where the pain was.

Ready, Trina? he said.

Hmm. But I don't feel well.

What's the matter?

How do I know? I'm just very tired today.

We're only going for a drive—you won't have to walk. The fresh air will do you good.

No lack of fresh air in your flat.

No, no, come along, please. I hate it in this flat.

Why? It's quite nice.

I don't know why. I can't stay in here too long.

Making the sound of laughter, Trina said, Will I hate it here, too, Deb?

No. You won't. I react to certain things this way. You know everything, don't you? There are all these bitter memories, the loneliness . . . I feel suffocated sometimes. Robi did too.

What was Robi saying about haunted houses, Deb?

He's a child, after all, Someone's scared him, saying that his mother is still here as a ghost.

Trina was silent for a bit. Then she said suddenly, When he telephoned this afternoon, Robi had asked me, Who are you—Ma?

What did you say?

What could I say? Wrong number, I lied.

Just as well.

Did he think his mother's ghost had answered the phone? Debashish laughed loudly. Yes, he said. My son's crazy.

Listen.

What?

Let's go out a little later. I need to sit down for a bit. I feel dizzy.

Taking Trina's hand, Debashish gently helped her to the sofa. Sitting next to her, he held her wrist, saying, Your pulse is quite weak.

Leaning her head back, Trina said, It's not a good day today. It's a horrible day.

Why, Trina? asked Debashish, leaning over her anxiously.

Trina raised her hand to stop Debashish's face from coming closer. You have these days, she said, when everything you do, from the morning onwards, goes wrong. As though you're possessed by a spirit.

How do you mean?

For instance, I never go into Manu or Reba's rooms these days. Today, I seemed to be possessed. I went. Reba turned up suddenly, and I was caught like a thief. How terribly she behaved.

You love Reba so much, Trina.

So much. That's why she breaks my heart.

It's past seven, Trina.

What's the hurry? It's not just another day, is it? Everything has been topsy-turvy since morning. It's such a strange day. Forget the watch.

I will. Go on.

Then there was Manu. I'd told him, Help me to my room, I don't feel very well. The boy just picked me up in his arms. Normally he doesn't even talk to me. Why today, then . . .? Then Sachin. He was different, too, today. Picked up my hanky, said a lot of things . . .

Listen, Trina, we haven't telephoned Sachin yet.

Later.

By now they must be wondering where you are. Why make them worry unnecessarily?

Let them. Let them worry. They never do.

No, Trina. You're wrong. Whatever you do, do it with conviction. You're not a thief.

Taking Debashish's hand, Trina said, You have too many fears. Listen to me.

Debashish exhaled. Tell me.

I was possessed as soon as I left home.

How do you mean?

I took the wrong road. Only when somebody rode past on a motorcycle did I come to my senses. Then I went the wrong way again. A taxi took me to Deshapriya Park. I didn't remember I had to give him directions, didn't even notice which way he was taking me. That's why I keep thinking it's a very strange day.

What do you mean, Trina?

Trina looked at him in the darkness. You have these days that start with mistakes, she said, and end with mistakes too. Haunted days.

No, Trina, it's not ending with a mistake. You're too old-fashioned.

No, Deb. You know, I've done just the one thing right today.

What?

Not telling Sachin before I left.

You should have. *That* was the mistake.

Trina shook her head. No. Telling him would have been.

I'm telephoning Sachin again right now, said Debashish impatiently.

Debashish rose without paying attention to her protests. Leaning over the phone, he dialled, trying to identify the numbers in the low light.

He waited, receiver held to his ear. Going up to him, Trina took the receiver from his hand. She was about to disconnect, when a girl's voice said at the other end, Hello.

Reba, probably. Trina put the receiver to her ear.

Reba spoke in a restless, impatient, voice. Who is it? Hello? Who is it?

Trina didn't dare reply. She just listened.

Reba was calling out for her father, Bapi, see, the phone rang, but no one's answering.

Sachin's voice, the very next moment. Hello.

Trina covered the mouthpiece with her hand.

Ghost call, Sachin told Reba. So many problems with the phone these days.

For the last time, he said, Hello, who is it?

No one. I'm no one, Trina said in her head.

Bringing his lips near her ears, Debashish said kindly, Couldn't tell him, Trina?

Sachin disconnected.

Trina shook her head. No. Not today. It's not a good day, Deb.

It's a very good day Trina.

No, Deb, today's not a day for decisions.

In that case, what'll you do, Trina?

In that case . . .

Trina frowned as she pondered. She pondered for a long time.

Debashish waited in eager anticipation.

The car stopped. The car drove away.

Trina stood alone before her house. In her heart she felt a void, like a huge expanse of empty sky. Only vultures of dread circling in it.

It was past eight at night. But not very late, of course. She could walk in quite easily. Nobody would even spare her a glance because of the lateness of the hour. Debashish's car reached the end of the road and turned left.

Trina walked in through the gate with slow steps. A bright light shone outside. There was a breeze. The moon was up. The breeze carried the fragrance of flowers in waves.

Trina had begged Debashish to grant her a day's reprieve. Today was not a good day. She was not up to such a monumental act of courage on a haunted day such as this one. Once this day had gone by, she could leave any other day that she wanted to. Why would she stay here? Why would she!

Slowly, she took the stairs to the first floor. Reba and a South Indian friend of hers named Saraswati were playing table tennis in the room on the left. They were running around, laughing. Nobody saw her.

Sachin's parrot cried, Stop thief! Stop thief! Stop thief! Sachin! Sachin! Sachin!

Trina slowly entered her room. She didn't switch on the light. Sitting silently on her bed for some time, she sensed the sky within her breast, the vultures circling. She would have written a poem about it had she been in the right frame of mind.

Trina fell asleep at some point, without even realizing it herself. The servant appeared to call her, Ma, don't you want dinner? Everyone's waiting.

Trina got up. The servant's addressing her as Ma kept ringing in her ears. After visiting the toilet, she went to the dining table. She was almost always present at dinner. Habit. No harm would be caused by her absence. But still, it was habit.

Everyone around the dining table was in a good mood.

Sachin was telling stories to the children. Religious fables. Everyone was listening. Not that Trina was ever included. She sat quietly at one side of the table. The food was laid out. Everyone helped themselves.

Finishing his story, Sachin said, Wait till the consignment from Japan arrives. What a bonsai garden we'll have.

They teach ikebana at school, said Reba.

What on earth is that? asked Manu.

Flower arrangement. It's great fun. The Japanese arrange flowers in the patterns of heaven, humans and earth. Amazing.

The Japanese are very advanced, aren't they, Baba? asked Manu.

Very advanced, said Sachin. No one is as clever as they are either. Just that they're too sentimental—they commit suicide at the drop of a hat.

Harikiri, said Reba.

Not harikiri. Harakiri, said Manu.

The conversation ran along these lines.

The cook stood silently in one corner, as he did every day. He was an excellent cook. Never made a mistake.

Today, however, as soon as she had had her first spoonful of the Chinese chop suey, Reba shouted, You forgot the salt, Chitto.

But I didn't forget, said Chitto, galvanized.

You did, said Reba aggressively.

Trying a spoonful, Manu said, He didn't forget entirely, but there's not enough salt.

But it's delicious, said Sachin.

Reba passed the salt cellar to her father in irritation. Then she decided to sprinkle the salt on his plate herself. And on Manu's, too.

Then suddenly she turned to Trina, saying, Ma, what about you? . . . Oh, you haven't even started!

Trina could not believe her ears. She simply could not

believe that Reba had just addressed her as Ma. She had not done that for a year. Her face and ears began to throb as the blood surged into them. Her heart was swept away, her soul eroded. After aeons, her breasts seemed full with milk. Overwrought, she gripped the handles of her chair hard. Joy! Joy! It was as though she had never felt such joy before. No one noticed her. Just as well! Sachin was telling them a story about something that had happened abroad. Did they even know that a torrent had been unleashed within her? A waterfall cascaded through her body ceaselessly, soaking everything nearby, Trina listened closely to its roar.

The next morning Trina sat down with her poetry notebook.

Today, too, Debashish would come. In the afternoon. To the bus stop.

Chandana's ghost was roaming around the house all day.

Debashish smoked by himself for a long time. He rose again, leaning out of the window towards the road below. The pavement was a long way down. In between lay the yawning emptiness. How had Chandana summoned up so much courage?

Debashish could not. Calcutta was flooded by moonlight. He had brought flowers to decorate the room, for their first night together. Now that fragrance had spread everywhere. How lovely the fragrance was! It held him back.

Debashish sat alone on the sofa like a spectre, clutching his hair in his hands. Robi wasn't here. Robi was sleeping deeply, snuggling up to his Monima.

Debashish went into Robi's room—as he did every night. Robi breathed quickly when he slept. He would look at him. Tuck him in. Tonight Robi's tiny bed was empty.

It was such a strange day. Debashish felt as surprised as a

child does when it discovers that the money it was holding in its fist is lost.

Robi was not there. Trina was not there.

Good. This was good in a way.

Debashish let out a horrible, dry laugh—like a spirit.

The bullet from Robi's toy-revolver still seemed to be lodged in his chest. Agony.

Debashish made a small sound, unable to understand the agony.

A big project of Indec's was getting underway the next day at Asansol. He would have to take a train at dawn.

Debashish went to bed. Sleep came in waves, like heavy fatigue. About to drop off, he remembered mistakenly telling Trina to come to the bus stop tomorrow. She would have to go back.

Should he telephone her now? Forget it. Today was a day of mistakes. He would not try to correct them today. Let them be. Let this day of mistakes go by.